THE ISLAND

KRIS LEITH

Paperback: 978-1-965632-61-1
eBook: 978-1-965632-62-8
Library of Congress Control Number: 2024922687

Ordering Information:

Prime Seven Media
518 Landmann St.
Tomah City, WI 54660

Printed in the United States of America

Dedication

I'd like to dedicate this book
to my family and friends.
I hope you enjoy it.

CHAPTER 1

It's late, but I can feel the intensity beginning to rise. The DJ kicks the beat up a notch sending the crowd into over-drive. It's near total madness on the dance floor. Masses of bodies ebb and flow to a rhythm that assaults them from the darkness. Black lights hang from the ceiling pulsing an invisible glow that makes fluorescent colours flash in dazzling brightness.

People are everywhere, bumping, grinding, pushing into each other.

I shake my head.

The pulse from the huge speakers is beginning to give me a headache. Hopefully I won't be here long. This is not my scene and people are beginning to stare sideways at me.

I turn my attention to the door on the far side of the bar, I can barely see it. If my contact hadn't told me about it then I would have never found it.

It's painted black and sits flush to the wall.

My thoughts flick back to the body in the morgue. She had just celebrated her eighteenth birthday, it was the day after she was found floating face down in Tauranga harbour, a port city on the east coast of New Zealand.

A police dive boat recovered her body from the water. She had no identification on her but a group of people came forward about a missing person. They told the police that her name was Jackie. She was blond, five foot six.

They had last seen her in the Rossi bar. She walked out with someone she had been dancing with. One of her friends tried to catch her but lost her in the midnight crowd. Jackie's friend then returned to the Rossi Bar.

They decided to wait to see if she returned.

I lowered my gaze to the floor; someone leaned in close and yelled something in my ear. I slowly looked up and saw a big guy standing next to me.

He wasn't my contact.

I played dumb and pretended not to hear what he had said. I put my hand up to my ear, with a confused expression on my face I mouthed the word 'what'.

The guy looked down at me, obviously not impressed that he had to tell me twice to either buy a drink or leave. I waited for him to lean in again then I grabbed him by his shirt collar and pulled him off balance. He fell forward planting two hands either side of me and braced himself against the bar. I leaned in so my nose was millimetres away from his. I glanced down and flashed my fake badge so only he could see.

He looked down then back up. The fight went out of him and he stopped struggling. I leaned forward to yell at him.

"I suggest you forget that you ever met me. Unless you have something you desperately want to tell me?"

He shook his head and tried to push himself away.

I held him in place a second longer, then let him go.

I wanted him to know that I was in control.

He backed away then stopped.

I thought for a moment that he was about to do something stupid, but he didn't. I guess he didn't want the wrath of management coming down on him. He turned then disappeared into the crowd.

I looked at my watch, it was twenty past midnight. The music was getting louder and faster and I was getting absolutely sick of the noise. I decided to wait another ten minutes for my contact to show, if he didn't I would deal with him tomorrow.

I turned to the bar deciding to buy something after all.

Scanning the shelf behind the bar, I saw they had everything from single malt whiskeys through to tap beer.

I waited for one of the bar ladies to look my way. I caught her eye and she walked briskly over. I leaned across the bar to yell at her. She leaned in closer, obviously not hearing what I was saying so I gave up and pointed at a bottle of imported beer in the fridge behind her. She looked back then removed it from the shelf and had the top off in one swift well practiced movement.

She leaned across the bar to yell at me.

"Nine dollars." She near screamed.

I placed a ten on the bar and waved away the change. She smiled at me and mouthed thank you. Someone was making a lot of money from young people tonight. I ran my finger around the top of the bottle then glanced at the mirrored wall behind the bar. My contact was standing behind me. He grinned as I turned around. He leaned in close and yelled something that was lost in the hideous thump of the music.

I pointed at my ear and shook my head.

He turned and waved me towards the near invisible door.

Chapter 2

Amy Tarrant was in her final year of university. She was studying chemistry and her future promised to be very exciting. With all her exams passed, she was placed in the top percentile of students for the last ten years. Already a handful of job opportunities and career offers had been made available to her that she would have to consider.

Her parents were urging her towards a medical career as a surgeon but in her mind that was of no interest.

Her focus was more aligned with research and development, finding and developing new antidotes and drugs.

A particular challenge she wanted to take on was finding a cure for the common cold. An exhaustive amount of research had already been undertaken by various people from around the world, but she wanted to be involved. She thought the ideas she had would be worthy of recognition.

First off though, she had to pass her final test.

Or *the* final test as the tutors put it.

She folded her text book closed and slipped it in to her pack. She picked the pack up from the floor; it was heavier to normal. Amy slipped the thin strap over her shoulder and instantly it dug in causing pain to shoot through her skin.

She adjusted it, eventually getting it comfortable enough for the short walk home.

Amy, and her friend Karen lived in the city, with Karen's cat Ginger. Karen and Amy had been friends for a long time, but Ginger had steadfastly refused any friendly advances from Amy.

The scratches on her arms during the first number of weeks were a testament to that.

Amy stepped out of the lecture hall and walked towards the main campus. She had a date tonight, Karen had promised to style her hair. While normally she wouldn't have bothered, Amy wanted to make an impression. She had meet Robert in an internet chat room. They had clicked straight away, or as much as anyone could in a virtual chat room.

She waited a few minutes outside then saw Karen stepping slowly down the steps from her physics lecture, Amy waved causing Karen to shift course and head in her direction.

"You're going to be angry with me." Karen said quietly looking up at her.

"Why, what have you done now?" Amy asked.

"I have to work late, sorry."

Amy dropped her shoulders. She guessed her hair would have to stay as it was for tonight's date.

"Ok. I guess I can fumble through tonight with this." She replied grabbing a handful of hair inspecting the split ends.

"Sorry, but Harvey is really working us. I swear she doesn't like anyone younger than herself." Karen stated, looking across some of the university buildings.

Amy nodded; she knew what the old bat was like.

"Lunch?" She asked looking at her hopefully.

Karen looked back at Amy, hesitated then nodded her agreement.

Together they headed towards the campus cafeteria.

CHAPTER 3

· ·

The noise deadened somewhat as the door slammed shut behind me. But the thud of the insane base still hit me in the chest. It wasn't until my contact turned and talked to me that I realised just how loud it was out in the club. I placed my hands over my ears to instantly hear the tell tale sign of tinnitus. I dropped my hands to my sides.

"How much do you want to buy?" He asked again.

I pulled a wad of cash from my pocket. It was a roll of one hundred dollar notes, I held it up in front of his face. His eyes lit up then I stuffed it back into my pocket, my contact's eyes never leaving the roll of cash.

"Let's just say if I like it then there is a lot more of where that came from."

He cleared his throat; up until this point we had never referred to each other by name, which suited me but now he was going to break that rule.

"My name is Hammond. Most people just call me Harry. We aren't usually in the business of dealing locally, but for the right person my associates can make an exception. Of course, you will have to prove to us that we can trust you. I am sure you are aware that there are a lot of people who would like to see us go down." Harry stated.

I was sure he had just threatened me, that is one thing that I will not endure.

I stepped forward until I was inches from him and gazed hard into his eyes.

"If you have any intention of messing with me Harry, I will ensure personally, that every single one of you and your so called associates are wiped off the face of the planet." I whispered just loud enough to be heard above the thump of the background noise.

I watched Harry's eyes intently, the reassuring lump of the Beretta in the small of my back.

He backed down.

Harry swallowed a bubble of air; this was the first time he had been on the receiving end of a threat. Usually he was the one barking instructions and looking tough. Harry nodded then looked away. When he spoke his voice was noticeably strained.

"This way." He squeaked.

I watched him turn to walk down a long hallway towards the rear of the building. He reached a door at the end then removed a single key from his pocket and slipped it into the lock. He turned the handle, pushed the door open then stepped to the side.

I took the cue and walked through the door into a drearily lit room.

It was quiet; the thump of the bass had receded to almost nothing, it had been replaced by a soft voice that eminated from hidden speakers in the back ground. Harry stepped in behind me then closed and locked the door.

There were three people in the room. Two wore jackets covered in patches; I could plainly see pistols in holsters hidden under their arms. They wore wrap around sun glasses even though the room was dull.

Neither of them moved when I walked in. They were your standard type of bodyguard. Daunting to look at, which is all that is usually needed but not really the fighting type, hence the pistols.

The third person however, I knew instantly by looking at him that he was going to be a handful. He was a muscle bound gorilla that had been jacked up on steroids since birth. The guy's hands were like a bunch of over ripe bananas. The muscles supporting his massive head made his neck almost nonexistent.

He stepped forward, towering over me, looked down at me then at Harry.

"He's here about a purchase." Harry told him.

The hairy ape looked down at me again then turned and walked for the door at the end of the room. It had a gold plaque on it with some fine black writing etched into its surface but it was too far to read. The giant lifted a huge hand, knocked once then turned the handle and walked into the dark office.

He didn't bother closing the door.

"There is someone here to see you." The giant stated, his voice high and taut from far too many steroids for far too long.

I eyed the two standing in opposite corners of the room. They hadn't shifted a muscle but I knew they were watching every move I made. The giant turned and walked back into the room followed by another smaller man. He closed the door behind himself then headed for a chair along the adjacent wall. He didn't make eye contact with me until he was settled and comfortable.

"My associate here tells me that you are willing to purchase a large quantity." The man said nodding at Harry.

I held the man's gaze and said nothing.

"Tell me, why I should sell to you when I am already doing so well. I really don't have any need of your services." The man stated matter-of-factly.

I smiled then looked down at the cheap tacky carpet.

"Well that is your decision. All I can tell you is that I would be able to double your profits within a year, if the price and product is of the quality you say it is." I replied equally as calm.

I watched him closely, his reaction was very subtle but I knew I had his interest.

The man in the seat watched me carefully then looked up at the giant.

"Has anyone patted him down?" He asked, pointing at me.

The giant looked down at the man in the chair then stepped forward quickly and began to roughly frisk me. He found the pistol and pulled it from the holster. It was loaded but a round wasn't chambered, I wasn't expecting trouble tonight but it looked like I may have misjudged the situation.

The giant handed the man in the seat the pistol. He studied it, turning it over in his hands.

"Nice piece. Normally I don't let anyone come in here armed, I guess procedures will have to be……amended." The man shot Harry and the two bikers a look.

I guessed that could only mean bad news.

"Now why don't you tell me how you intend to double my profit and what exactly you expect in return?" He stated calmly as he placed the pistol on his knee.

I looked at the giant then down at the man in the seat.

I figured I could get across the room in two large steps and use the momentum to drive my foot into the man' chest. He was against a wall so his ribs would crack instantly like dried twigs. In that position the giant was blocking one of the guys in glasses from view but the other had a clear shot.

It also put me a little to close for comfort to the giant.

I relaxed, then ran through what I had rehearsed. When I had finished my pitch the man remained unmoved. I had noticed the two in glasses turn to look at me when I divulged some details but other than that there was no reaction.

The man stood, looked at me for a second, then turned and walked into his office followed by the giant.

I turned and glanced at Harry; he shrugged his shoulders then looked back at the door as it swung open again. The giant stepped out then closed the door. He walked up to me and handed me an envelope.

"Be here at the time stated." He told me in his high pitched voice, then turned and walked back into the office.

The two guys with glasses walked up to me to stand between me and the door. One guy stepped past and opened the door behind me to the hallway. Thumping music flooded into the room again, I could feel my headache click up a notch.

"Don't let the door hit you in the ass on the way out." The guy in front of me taunted.

I stopped in the doorway and turned, acutely aware that I didn't get my Beretta back.

Deciding not to reply, I walked slowly towards the door that led back into the club and the thumping noise.

Chapter 4

I stepped out onto the street after pushing my way through the crowd. My headache was getting worse and I dreaded the coming morning.

The water front and surrounding streets were flooded with people. It looked like half the town had converged on The Strand for Friday night.

The day was nothing special; it was usually like this during the weekend. Slowly, I walked towards The Strand; the night was cold but not winter cold yet. The sidewalks teemed with masses of people moving from one bar to another, in the doorways stood bouncers, there to keep the undesirables out.

I had turned the corner and saw a van parked in a loading zone. It didn't matter though, I wasn't about to stop and tell him to move, I was sure I had a tail. I stepped past the van carrying on down the street, away from town and away from the crowds.

I followed the road as it wandered over a set of railway tracks that led to the ship yards and the harbour bridge. Broken clouds scattered moonlight across the land in front of me bathing areas in silver light and others in dark shadows. The road wound its way past an old lot of sheds, a used car lot then the side of the road was bare, just grass and manicured gardens. I stopped, pretending to check the time and listened for any footsteps behind me.

Nothing.

Still, I was certain someone was following me.

I carried on; the shadows grew deeper as I neared the bridge. I could hear the dull roar of cars passing overhead. I was swallowed up in the shadows which made the next part a lot easier to accomplish. Swiftly but quietly, I stepped off the path and headed for a small grove of trees near a hill that ran towards another part of town. Light hit the tops of the trees but the trunks were bathed in darkness. I slipped behind one then couched and turned to look back towards The Strand.

It took ten minutes before I saw someone come into view. The figure would take a few steps then stop and turn a full circle, take another few steps then another full circle.

I watched and waited.

It took another five minutes for the figure to become adjacent to me. Now the person was five metres away with their back turned looking out over the harbour. I stood silently, checking either way for traffic.

Slowly, I broke away from the tree and began to silently close the distance behind the figure. When I was a metre away, I leapt at the figure; my arms came up wrapping around the persons throat.

It was one of the guys from the club.

He had lost the glasses but still had the patched jacket on. He froze as soon as I locked my arms, then began to thrash when he realised what was going on. He wouldn't break the hold though; I had a good six inches in height on him and outweighed him by a good margin. The guy made a play for the pistol under his jacket but I was ready for it.

I leaned back and stretched upwards lifting the guy off the ground by his neck. He began to choke and claw at my arm.

"If you reach for the gun again, I'll break your neck, ok?" I whispered in his ear.

He struggled for a few more seconds then went limp. Slowly I let him down so his feet were on the ground but didn't let go of his neck.

"Why are you following me?" I asked.

They guy didn't answer so I asked him again.

"Why are you following me?" I whispered as I increased the pressure slowly.

The guy tried to twist around but I clamped my forearm across his throat and leaned back, he stopped moving.

"Harry told me to make sure you got home." He said in a rasp.

I grinned.

"Don't believe you." I said as I lifted him off the ground again.

"Ok, Ok." He gasped.

I let him down again, but didn't let him go.

"Ok, no more games. Tell me why you were following me or you're going for a swim."

"John told me to follow you, didn't say why." He choked out.

"Who's John and why didn't he tell you?" I asked.

"The boss, we don't question him." He rasped.

"Don't you think you have the right to know what you are getting yourself in for; I mean you could be walking into a trap." I began to relax my grip.

"Now, I am going to let you go, all I want is some straight answers."
I stated politely.

The man stayed still for a second then nodded against my forearm.

Slowly I pulled my arms away, the guy with the patched jacket stepped away from me rubbing his throat. I could read the patch in the silver moonlight. He belonged to a gang.

"Now, tell me why John told you to follow me." I stated.

The biker turned to face me.

"You dont need to know that, asshole." He spat with a grin.

I nodded.

"We had a deal. That deal still stands." I told him.

The biker leaned forward as if he were trying to intimidate me. Obviously a tactic he had used before which had drawn the desired reaction.

He was out of reach so I lunged at him. Two hundred and twenty pounds of muscle launched at him like a rocket. He tried to lean back to get away but wasn't quick enough. I grabbed the lapels of his jacket landing squarely on his chest. We crashed to the ground, I heard the wind escape his lungs and his eyes bulged.

"Last chance." I yelled.

The guy flailed his arms uselessly, I realised that he was trying to say something. I pulled his pistol from its holster then stepped off him. The biker rolled around on the ground gasping for breath.

"It would be a lot less painful for you if you just told me what you know." I said as I looked at the pistol in the moon light.

I pulled the slide back; there was a round in the chamber so I let it slam home.

The biker rolled onto his back and looked up at me as he clutched his chest.

"John told me to follow you, see where you lived." The biker finally answered when he got his breath back.

I looked down at the pathetic punk.

"Why?" I asked.

"Why what?" The biker replied.

I pulled the pistol up levelling it at the man's forehead.

"Whoa, hey man, take it easy. I just got told to follow you and tell them where you live, that's all, I swear." The biker pleaded.

I cocked the hammer then crouched down placing the muzzle against the guy's forehead. He tried to back away but I drove the muzzle down until he was lying on the ground, the gun pointing straight down.

"Now, if you're messing with me, I will find you." I whispered.

The guy shook his head.

"I'm not lying man." He answered.

I uncocked the hammer then stood up slowly. I looked up the road. It would have been hard for anyone to see us if they drove past, which thankfully no one did.

Slowly I stepped back and began pulling the pistol to pieces. I dropped the magazine into my jacket pocket then threw the remaining parts across the road into the harbour.

"Ok you can come in now." I spoke quietly.

The guy on the grass looked up at me with a confused look. I looked down at him then grabbed his jacket and lifted him off the ground.

"Now I want you to tell John that if he wants to do business then that's great, we stand to make a lot of money, both of us. You can also tell him that I don't appreciate being followed, anywhere. Got it?" I asked.

The biker nodded. We both looked towards The Strand as a set of lights turned slowly down the road. I pulled the guy across the grass towards the road then carried on towards the harbour. It was only three feet deep near the rock wall.

The biker realised what was about to happen and began to struggle, I clamped my fingers harder around his jacket then began to run towards the rock wall pulling the guy off balance. I stopped suddenly letting momentum do the rest of the work for me. The biker managed to stop on the edge of the rocks but not in time.

He teetered for a second, then fell in as the van pulled up on the opposite side of the road.

I smiled then turned and walked to the waiting van.

Chapter 5

John screwed a suppressor onto a small silver pistol. It was a gift from his father. He had shown John how to use it and John had become a very talented marksman with it.

John realised the value of a pistol, in his eyes it was almost the perfect weapon for personal protection. He placed it carefully on the desk in front of him then selected one of the two chrome magazines from the mahogany box. He opened a fresh box of nine millimetre parabellum rounds designed specifically for use with a suppressor. He removed a round and pushed it carefully into the magazine, followed by four more.

Gently he slid the magazine into the grip of the pistol, slowly pulled the slide back then let it slip forward stripping a round from the magazine driving it into the chamber.

He loved the way the small pistol felt in his hands, it was perfectly balanced. The German manufacturer was more than happy to supply it for the inflated price his father had brought it for. John's father didn't mind though, he knew precision craftsmanship when he saw it, as did John.

"You were told to follow him." John stated.

The biker visibly shook, more from fear than cold. Water pooled at his feet drenching the carpet. The biker didn't answer, instead he looked across the room at the giant standing in the corner next to John.

John spun in his seat and looked up at the giant. The giant understood what he wanted and slipped around the corner of the desk with surprising speed. Before the biker could protest, the giant had bunched the collar of his jacket in his fist.

The punch to the stomach sounded like a battering ram hitting a plump pillow. John smiled as the biker doubled over and fell to the floor gasping for breath. The giant turned then walked back around the desk and stood with his back against the wall again.

The gasping continued for a short while during which no one uttered a word; John cleared his throat waiting for the biker to recover.

The biker crawled to his knees as fast as he could, well aware that he was being watched and they were waiting for an answer.

"Mister Rossi, I lost him in the crowd. He slipped away, I couldn't find him again." The biker lied knowing that if he told the truth that he had been caught and thrown in the harbour, he would surely not see the night out.

The giant laughed, Rossi turned to look up at him.

"I see. So, would you care to tell me why you went for a swim then?" Rossi asked as he turned back to the biker.

The biker looked down and realised he didn't have an answer.

"Uh um…. I."

"You were thrown into the harbour by our friend Mister Blackstone. You see Robert, I have eyes everywhere, your incompetence has lost me the advantage. Not only do I want to know who he works for, I want to know where he lives, something that is obviously beyond the scope of your abilities, which makes me think I should terminate our agreement, don't you think?" Rossi asked.

Robert shook his head and nodded at the same time from the cold.

"Well. Yes or no?" Rossi asked again.

Robert began to panic, his mind raced to search for an answer. He wanted to prove he was capable and wasn't above grovelling for a second chance. He began to crawl forward on his knees until he reached the desk. He placed his hands on the hardwood top then began to plead his case.

Rossi looked down at the pathetic excuse in disgust. He raised his left hand to stop the biker from whining, while slowly leaning forward.

"I am afraid you have run out of chances." Rossi stated as he lifted the pistol off the desk.

Rossi extended his arm across the desk, brought the muzzle three inches from the biker's forehead then squeezed the trigger.

The pistol coughed and a plume of red mist arced from the back of the man's skull. Robert fell backwards on to the carpet in a crumpled heap. John turned to look at the giant.

"Get rid of that would you." He ordered.

The giant nodded and pulled a small cell phone from his pocket which all but disappeared in his oversized hand. The giant carefully punched in a number then talked quietly to the person on the other end of the line. He flipped it shut then looked down at Rossi.

"They will be here in twenty minutes." He reassured Rossi.

"Good, make sure you take him a long way out, we don't want him coming back anytime soon." The giant nodded then headed for the door.

Once the door had clicked shut John placed the silver pistol on the desk then removed a key from the inside pocket of his designer coat. It was for a locked draw in which he kept his most important documents. Rossi opened the draw to remove a piece of paper with a neat letter head embossed across the top. He read the number then dialled it into a phone he kept purely for this reason. It was a secure line that, if anyone were listening, would hear nothing but garbled static.

The phone clicked then began to ring.

"*Yes.*" The voice answered.

John waited a beat before he started.

"The shipment is being prepared as we speak." John spoke softly.

"*Good. Remember John, we do not tolerate failure.*" The electronic voice stated.

Rossi felt his heart skip a beat.

"We may have a solu...." He started but the voice cut him off.

"*Fill the order, John.*" Then the line went dead.

John slowly moved the receiver away from his ear and gazed at it with a panicked expression then dropped it onto the desk.

Chapter 6

"Do you think that was wise, I mean, he wasn't posing a threat?" Dan asked.

I turned to look across the van at him.

"Just concentrate on driving would you." I replied.

"He could have provided some interesting if not useful information. Did you get a name at least?" He asked again ignoring my request.

I rifled through the contents of the bikers wallet as Dan navigated the large van through the gorge on our way back to Auckland. The biker had a learner licence and a few hundred dollars in cash. I searched the rest of the wallet but found nothing of use.

"Guy's name is Robert Cane. He's got a learners licence even though he's thirty eight."

I flipped the licence over.

"And it's expired." I pushed the licence back into the wallet then dumped it on the seat beside me.

"Did you get anything useful?" I asked.

Dan shook his head.

"Not really. Just the name John which I assume is the leader of this operation." Dan stated.

I nodded but said nothing. We drove in silence as I thought about my next move.

"You have to go back; we don't have enough evidence yet." Dan stated quietly.

"Yeah, and next time I might not get away so easily. This guy is smart; he hasn't survived this long by being taken for a ride." I replied.

There had been a massive influx of foreign drugs arriving onto New Zealand shores resulting in numerous deaths. I closed my eyes and looked at John's face. His eyes spoke volumes to me. But Dan was right, I wasn't going to get anywhere by sitting on my hands.

"It has to be him." I whispered.

The comment was lost in the engine noise of the van.

I stayed quiet for the rest of the trip home. Dan reached the motorway and headed south towards Te Kauwhata.

It was early the next morning when I pushed the door open and stepped inside, I could only think about one thing as I flicked the light on in the hallway.

I turned the alarm off then fell onto the bed, before I knew it everything went dark.

I awoke the next morning to the sound of rain on the roof. It wasn't heavy but it sounded like it was here to stay. I wanted to research my new business partner some more. I was sure I would find something Dan had overlooked.

Climbing out of bed, I realised that no sun shone through the clouds; it was an abysmal day, I looked at my burner phone, no messages.

I turned on the computer and began trawling through newspaper clippings and forensics reports.

Chapter 7

The giant sat at the bow of the boat watching the water break against the hull. He enjoyed being at sea. It had a calming influence making him feel at peace. He had grown up around ship yards, his father had been a stevedore. When he was old enough, his father managed to persuade the company to offer him a job working alongside those he had grown up with. The giant, even back then was not small. The manager found him a useful associate when it came to negotiations with the unions, which consequently gained him the extra money he could only dream of.

His father didn't like him working for management, he told his son that the workers had to stick together and fight, there was strength in numbers. The giant knew what his father was saying but told him he knew what he was doing.

As time passed, the giant and his father became more and more distant from each other until they clashed at work during a protest. The father asked his son to step aside to allow the protestors to pass.

The giant looked down at his father with dead eyes, then hit him square on the forehead, sending him to hospital with permanent brain damage.

That was the beginning for the giant.

They had departed early in the morning to make sure they had enough time to get back before darness fell. It took nearly three hours to reach Mayor Island off the coast of Tauranga. It was a leisurely ride out during which the giant had dropped a line off the stern of the boat with a steel trace. He loved fishing, in particular big game fishing.

His favourite being Marlin.

But today he was after shark.

The giant's boat rod was specially designed for him, as was the reel. The deck hand dumped bucketful after bucketful of burly overboard in an effort to attract the oceans main predator.

The giant stood at the bow looking off across the ocean to the distant shore line. Dark threatening clouds hung over the Kaimai range, he knew the ride back was going to be rough. He turned then walked to the rear of the boat to sit in the chair anchored to the hull designed to play large fish. The giant watched the rod tip bob and bend under the speed of the boat. The view of the coast was spectacular. One day he would retire further east of Tauranga to a life of fishing and reading.

"We are fifteen minutes out." The Captain called from the top of the launch.

The giant turned and nodded at him then resumed watching the water.

The tip of the rod snapped down violently and the reel began to scream as line was yanked viciously from the oversize drum. The giant watched the line and followed it to the water to see if he could catch a glimpse of the fish. He stood then walked to the edge of the boat and gazed at the surface carefully.

"I think I've got one." He yelled behind him.

The Captain looked down and grinned as the deck hand came running out with a gaff. The reel stopped screaming and the line went slack as a big black fin broke the surface of the water then began heading towards the boat. The giant pulled the rod from the holder and sat back in the seat then began to reel the line in. Two smaller fins appeared as the Captain throttled back and the boat coasted around the eastern tip of the island.

As the giant wound the line in, it suddenly snapped taut again. He tightened the drag as the shark began to fight furiously. He smiled, the hook was set and the battle had begun. Multiple sets of fins began to break the surface and converge on the struggle. The giant looked at the deck hand and pointed at the large sack sitting against the corner of the boat.

"I think it's time." He called.

The deck hand opened the bag carefully to begin lifting the bikers severed limbs out then dropped them into the water. The surface of the ocean began to boil. The deck hand picked up the sack then upended it over the side. The giant didn't notice, he was focused on wrangling the shark.

"Its done Captain." The deck hand called.

The giant turned to look at the Captain who was watching the surface of the water foam with frothy red bubbles.

The giant felt the rod bend abruptly and the reel began to whine in protest, his head snapped back around in time to see the line disappear below the boat. He grabbed the reel and wound the drag on tighter to stop the furious descent. As the rod bent almost double he felt himself being dragged from the seat. The giant placed his feet against the deck rail and heaved backwards, his large arms straining, a grin on his face.

He was beginning to think he had bitten off more than he could chew; the boiling surface around the boat had all but ceased, only a few fish remained taking up the smaller pieces not taken by the sharks. Nothing was left behind.

The giant wound the drag on as tight as he could, slowing the reel to a crawl. The rod was now bent almost to the waters surface. The giant leaned back into the seat hoping the fight was going out of the fish, this was the most aggressive fight he'd had in a long time. The giant renewed his grip on the rod gripping it further up the stem then heaved back. The line popped and he fell heavily back into the chair.

"Damn it." The giant cursed.

The Captain shook his head in disbelief.

"Looks like today isn't your day."

CHAPTER 8

Nick Baker, loved his job. He had wanted more than anything, ever since he was young, to join the police force and clean up the city streets.

He had excelled in the training college; the instructors had told him that he could expect to go far with his kind of attitude.

He was tough but fair, or so he thought, the scar tracking down the left side of his torso told the tale that someone thought otherwise.

He remembered the night well.

Nick and his partner Catherine were walking the beat in south Auckland. They were on foot patrol because there had been a spate of burglaries and the Mayor had called for the police to do something about it. So the Captain had put more police on the street as a show of force, to reassure the public that they were there and had their best interests in mind.

Catherine was killed and Nick left for dead, the knife wound missing all his vital organs. The doctors couldn't explain it; they told him that by rights, he should have died on the street that night.

During his recovery Nick vowed to catch the person responsible, he wanted to make sure that the person was brought to justice.

The papers told of a man found mutilated and dismembered. It was a gruesome story with an equally gruesome ending. He wanted to send a message to the scum who committed such crime that there would be dire consequences for their actions.

It didn't have the effect Nick had hoped for.

Nick returned to work eager to get back to the serious crime unit, but to his dismay, he had been reassigned to traffic duty.

His disgust was evident but he stuck to it.

He spent a lot of time on the road, pursuing speeders and directing traffic.

Nick found the state of the country going from bad to worse and couldn't help but feel that he was headed in the same direction. He had not seen a pay raise in what seemed like forever which made him bitter towards the government in general and the police force in particular.

While patrolling the highways south of Auckland, he was passed by a car travelling nearly twice the legal limit. Nick slammed the throttle of his squad car down to the floor to give chase and soon had a dark coloured late model Porsche pulled over on the hard shoulder south of Mercer. He carefully noted down the plate number and gathered the necessary paperwork to hand to the idiot behind the wheel. But before he had a chance to step from the patrol car, the door of the Porsche swung open and out stepped a tall, athletically built man dressed in an impeccable suit. He slammed the door shut then casually walked to the rear of the porsche and leaned back against the wing watching Nick.

Nick stepped from his patrol car and roared at the man to get back in his car and put his belt on. Nick didn't really care that the man had stepped from his car or if he got flattened by another motorist, as far as he was concerned the road would be better off without people like him.

"What seems to be the problem officer?" The man asked casually.

Nick stepped up to him and made himself as tall as possible to gain the upper hand.

"Your speed. You were travelling almost twice the limit. You want to explain why?" Nick barked back.

The man just stood there staring at Nick, not saying a word.

"Well?" Nick asked again.

The man smiled then turned and walked back to his car.

"That is none of your concern. However I have something I wish to offer you." The man said as he opened the door and reached for his briefcase.

The man in the suit placed it on the bonnet of the Porsche, scratching the paint, which he ignored, and opened the lid. Inside there was a wad of papers and some business cards.

"What would you say, officer, if I told you that I could double, even triple your salary every year for the rest of your life, all you had to do was send me information?" The man asked as he handed him a card.

Nick looked down at the name on the card but didn't take it from him.

"I'd say I'm not interested sir, and you're under arrest; now turn around." He said as he laid a hand on the man.

The man in the suit didn't move.

"First of all, don't address me with that attitude, my name is John Rossi or in your case Mister Rossi; and second, you have exactly two seconds to remove your hand." The man stated in a quiet voice, although Nick could sense a deadly edge to it.

Nick didn't remove his hand; instead he just grinned and moved to turn the man around. What took place next defied logic; Nick wouldn't comprehend it until much later when he realised that John Rossi was much more dangerous than he gave him credit for.

As Nick turned Rossi around, the man side stepped and spun with him. Before Nick could stop moving Rossi was on top of him pushing his face into the bonnet of the Porsche with what felt like the muzzle of a pistol.

"Now you listen to me Nick Baker, that's right, I know all about you and where you and your young blonde wife live." Nick froze.

"You are going to do exactly as you are told. You will give me the information when and where it is required, do you understand?" Rossi asked.

"You can't do this!" Nick protested.

"I am an officer of the law." He said as Rossi drove the pistol harder into his neck.

"Yes, so I have been told. I also know about other deals you have going on, deals involving, oh lets say, undue reward for services rendered." Rossi paused.

"You see Nick; I am a businessman as I am sure you are. All I want is a little information every now and then, and if you come through, then you will be handsomely rewarded for it, which I am sure you are use to, right?" Rossi asked.

Nick stopped struggling completely and Rossi stepped back. Nick stayed slumped over the bonnet. Getting paid for sex or looking the other way for the odd blowjob was one thing but eliciting information for someone who was obviously a gangster, or worse, was an entirely different ballgame. Nick pushed himself off the bonnet of the Porsche and turned slowly around.

"But make no mistake Nick, if you try to cook me in any way, I will kill your family and make you watch then you will experience more pain than you could ever imagine possible." Rossi stated darkly.

Nick thought about his wife and what this animal would do to her if he tried something stupid.

"You're bluffing." Nick stated in one last final attempt to gain the upper hand.

Rossi just smiled at him then reached into his pocket. He removed a photograph and held it close to his chest so Nick couldn't see it.

"I can assure you Mister Baker, I am not joking." Rossi stated with a hint of an accent. Rossi looked down at the photo then showed it to Nick.

"You see Nick, the combination of your job and behaviour is of valued interest to me. I think we may be able to help each other significantly, don't you?" Rossi asked.

Nick couldn't believe what he was seeing or what he was about to say. The photo showed him in a compromising position with no less than three ladies. If he remembered correctly it was more like seven, but he never thought the photos would be used as leverage. Rossi showed him another photograph, this time he was snorting cocaine from a prostitute's breast.

"I don't think this is correct behaviour for a police officer, is it? I mean, if your wife found out about your exploits, you could lose your marriage, but you are far more important than that, aren't you Nick?" Rossi asked again.

"I…I… how did you get that?" Nick stammered.

"That is none of your concern, Nick. What is your concern is what you can do for me." Rossi stated.

Nick's jaw dropped open then closed again.

"First of all, you can forget about the ticket; second, you can get back in your car and drive back to the station. When you get there I want you to go straight to the Captain's office and tell him you want a desk job. I will call you at the end of the week; if you don't have a desk job by then these photos will be published on the front page of The Herald. Do you understand?" Rossi asked.

Nick's jaw dropped open and stayed open.

"Do you understand me, Nick?" Rossi asked in a raised voice.

Nick just nodded.

"But what if I can't get a desk job?" He squeaked.

"That isn't my concern Nick." Rossi grinned as he stepped close to him.

He carefully placed the pictures in the officer's top pocket and patted it flat.

"You can keep those Nick, keep it as a reminder that I am not lying and this isn't a bad dream." Rossi smiled at him then turned on his heel and stepped towards the drivers door.

"The end of the week Nick, I'll be in touch." Rossi called to him as he closed the door.

The engine fired then Rossi slammed his foot down hard leaving two black lines snaking along the shoulder and onto the road with Nick standing behind him watching him go.

Rossi's words echoed in Nick's mind.

It was a Tuesday afternoon.

Chapter 9

Dan looked across the table at me.

"What?" I asked as I put my cup down.

"You still miss her, don't you?" He asked back.

I rolled my eyes.

"No, I don't." I told him flatly.

Dan stayed quiet.

"She's gone, end of story. Can we move on?" I told him more than I asked.

Dan said nothing as I continued flicking through the sports section of the paper. The national cricket team had failed to fire once again, falling victim to a nation that should have made for a good match. Instead, the series was a white wash. I closed the paper, and looked across the table.

"We have some recon to do. I want to know who that giant is and I want to know more about the gang he has working for him. I'm going to set a meeting with John to formalise our arrangement." I stated.

Dan looked up from another section of the news paper.

"I assume you know he is going to want to meet the buyers at the other end." Dan told me.

I looked at him and nodded.

"He's going to snoop around to make sure you aren't full of it." He pointed out.

I nodded again but said nothing.

"You're making a mistake by rushing into it too soon. We don't even know if this guy is legit, he might be some crackpot thinking he's big." Dan stated.

I said nothing as I picked up my cup and took a sip.

"Ok, what do you suggest we do then?" I asked once I had placed the cup on the table.

"Like you said, recon. But let's look at who he is dealing with first. Find out exactly what we are getting into. If it's a cartel then things could spiral out of control very, very fast."

Emma handed the wad of cash to the guy she knew only by his first name. She was absolutely sure it wasn't his real name but then she didn't have to live with him so she didn't really care. The roll of bank notes was a lot of money for her.

Her usual buy was around a hundred dollars a time, more than enough for her to get high and enjoy her girlfriend. But she had heard that there was a new drug out, one that was supposed to be ten times the high than she was accustomed to.

Emma handed over the role of money totalling a thousand dollars, then the mystery man handed her a small plastic bag half full of white powder.

The man dropped it into her open palm then looked at her.

"Don't take this all at once, ok. This stuff is strong, ok, it'll really mess you up, ok?" The man told her.

Emma wasn't really listening to him, she was more interested in the coming high.

Her eyes focused on the contents of the bag.

"Listen to me, Emma." The man said as he grabbed her by the shoulder.

"Be careful with that stuff." He said as he shook her gently.

Emma pulled away from the man; he was beginning to scare her.

She turned then walked quickly down the small alleyway and out onto the main road.

Emma had grown up in a small country town but left it for the city as soon as she had finished high school.

She left Morrinsville behind, wanting to make something of her life. Emma had dreams of becoming an actress. Ever since she was young she had been captivated with movies. It was a fantasy world she could lose herself in for hours at a time, leaving the boredom she endured in her wake.

When she realised that she wanted to be the person on the screen instead of just watching it, she gave everything she had towards pursuing that dream.

However, when she arrived in Auckland she soon realised how difficult it was going to be to break into that fantasy world.

No-one wanted to know her, she was either too tall or had the wrong hair colour or not the right look. In frustration Emma kept returning, she kept going back telling herself that something big was going to happen, that something was just around the corner.

To Emma's joy, something big did happen. She met Harry. Harry told her he was an entrepreneur. He had charisma and charm plus he was refreshingly taller than her.

The string of men she had dated where always shorter and their ego drove them to prove that they were bigger than they really were, which brought Emma to the edge of insanity.

She didn't care how short or tall they were, as long as they treated her with kindness.

But her words kept falling on deaf ears.

Until she met Harry.

He did listen, he made her feel special, in the whirlwind three months they were together he introduced her to people she would never have dreamed of meeting.

Then something went wrong, Harry introduced her to Marshall.

He was a film executive for a large company in America, thats what he told her.

Marshall told Emma that he was looking for fresh faces, someone that would be the star in their latest film that was going into production soon.

Emma was star struck when Marshall told her he could see her name in lights on Broadway.

Maybe even a star on the Hollywood walk of fame.

Emma couldn't believe her luck so she decided to pursue the movie with Marshall. She sold everything she owned and purchased an open ended ticket to Los Angeles where Marshall met her at the airport.

Emma thought it was unusual that the executive of the company was there to greet her but then surmised that he had seen a talent in her that no one had and wanted to protect his investment.

Emma climbed into the back of the rented limo where she was greeted by two blondes and a man with his hair tied back in a ponytail.

The door was slammed shut then the limo fought its way out of the airport and away from the stifling traffic.

Emma said nothing; she just sat on the leather seat feeling uncomfortable trying to avoid the occasional eye contact with the man opposite her. The two blondes chatted together as if no one else were in the car with them.

The limo drove for what seemed like hours until finally it bumped over a kerb and continued up a long snaking driveway.

The door opened and Emma was greeted by a short man with a very large, very expensive looking house behind him.

Emma stepped from the limo, the door slammed shut and it swung away down the driveway. The short man greeted her in a language she couldn't understand.

It soon became evident that Emma had made a huge mistake when Marshall had asked her to take her clothes off, he wanted to see her, assets, as he called it, she had balked and told him that she wasn't that kind of actress.

Marshall laughed at her then asked her what exactly she was doing here. Emma's answer just made him laugh harder.

She waited for him to stop, her jaw set and a firm belief that she was right. Marshall apologised then offered her a drink. Begrudgingly she accepted.

When she woke up her clothes were gone and she was handcuffed to a bed.

She could hear people moving in the background and began to struggle.

Suddenly a hand pushed her onto the bed followed by a sharp sting that shot down her arm. Within seconds she felt light headed as if she was starved of oxygen, but she didn't care.

It felt great.

Emma remained on the bed for twelve hours as three different people poked and prodded her. She giggled a few times as they touched parts of her that tickled but other than that she didn't remember much.

What she did remember was the sting on her arm a few more times then nothing.

When Emma came to, her head thumped worse than anything she had ever felt, and a craving that only became worse the more she ignored it.

Her skin began to itch, she couldn't think clearly.

Alone she wandered the streets of LA for a week but she realised much sooner that she was hooked on heroin.

Emma began to panic but the craving eventually pushed the panic aside. Digging into the pockets of the clothes she had been wearing for a week, she realised that she had no money and nowhere to turn.

All she had to her name was her passport and the ticket back to New Zealand.

When she arrived in Auckland she was too ashamed to call her family, they knew nothing about her drug addiction. It consumed her thoughts, every waking moment; the only peace she could find was when she fell asleep.

Emma chose to stay in Auckland instead of returning home, she lied to her parents, telling them that they were filming on closed sets then she would be returning to Los Angeles.

Her acting career was really taking off.

But the real reason was she could get a better quality of heroin in Auckland, it was hard to come by at the best of times, but she knew somebody.

During a moment of clarity, Emma found she was more attracted to woman than men. If she examined her life carefully, she found evidence to back this up.

Her girl friends had been just that, her friends, while the men in her life had always tried to control her, made her feel inferior or physically and mentally abused her.

She swore herself off men, then met Elizabeth, an English girl on a mission to prove to her parents that she could make it by herself.

She was in just as much trouble as Emma, but together they managed to live.

Emma turned onto the main road that would take her back to their dingy dark apartment. It was in a bad part of town but they couldn't afford anywhere else. She picked her way towards one of the many dormant volcanos spotted around the greater Auckland district then turned up her street. Her legs moved quickly as she shuffled home, the weight of the contents in her pocket reminding her of what was waiting.

Emma swung the door open then closed it quickly locking it with the dead bolt and chain. She ran up the stairwell to their bedroom and burst through the door.

Elisabeth wasn't there.

"Liz, I'm back." She called down the stairwell.

No answer.

Emma shrugged her shoulders and headed back into the room. She carefully removed a small mirror from the set of draws by her bed and placed it on top next to the lamp.

Emma set about carefully measuring out half each then slid Elizabeth's portion back into the small bag. She looked down at the mirror screwing her nose up, it wasn't very much. Carefully she loaded her half of the powder into a spoon and held it over a flame until it boiled.

The cravings were beginning to creep up on her again.

Emma watched the solution bubble with anticipation. Just the sight of the dirty coloured liquid began to make her cravings relax, but she knew all too well that they wouldn't leave until the needle was in her veins.

Emma took a fresh syringe from a packet then drew the drug into the tube taking care to expel the air. She found a vein in her left arm, carefully pushed the needle in then slowly drove the plunger home.

The rush hit her faster and harder than she expected.

It wasn't the nice sensation she was used to. Her eyes fluttered and rolled back, her mind suddenly felt like it wasn't there, like it had been sucked into a dark bottomless void.

Emma stood on unsteady feet and put her hand against her forehead. She could feel hot flushes driving through her flesh.

The last thought she had was of her parents before she collapsed to the floor.

Chapter 10

Nick coasted through the streets of south Auckland in his squad car. His day was consumed by violence and drugs. He had lost count of how many call outs he had been to on this given day and his patience was beginning to wear thin dealing with it all. He occasionally thought about leaving the force, even leaving the country, but he knew he couldn't. He loved his job and the power it let him use against the scum of the country; then there was John Rossi.

Nick sighed deeply.

"What's wrong?" His partner Darren asked him.

Nick just shook his head keeping his focus on the street ahead of him. It was five o'clock in the afternoon and coming towards the end of his shift.

He rounded a corner to Manukau City then slowed as a set of lights changed to orange. He stopped second in line behind a people mover being used as the name suggested.

Nick's phone chirped and began to ring impatiently.

He pulled it from the holder buckled to his belt and flipped the screen open.

The number was blocked.

"Hello." He answered.

"Emery Blackstone, do you know him?" The voice asked.

Nick stuttered for a second.

"Never heard of the guy." Nick lied.

He had heard of him, in fact he had tailed the guy for a while but couldn't get anything on him.

"Then, Nick, we have a small problem." Rossi told him.

Nick froze in the seat, staring rigidly out the windscreen, the lights still red.

"Yes." He replied.

"I need you to find out about him. I've had a meeting with Blackstone, he is offering something that is a little too good to be true. I have told my people, they want me to make absolutely certain that nothing untoward will happen should we enter a business relationship with him. That is where you come in, Nick." The electronic voice stated.

Nick gulped a mouthful of air.

He wished every day that he had let the Porsche go and not bothered to give chase.

'That may be a little difficult." Nick replied carefully.

"I don't want to hear excuses. Dig up what you can on him. Don't let me down, Nick." Rossi threatened.

The line went dead, Nick clicked his phone shut.

"Who was that?" Darren asked.

"No one." Nick replied as he clicked the lights and sirens on.

He flashed his lights and slammed his palm against the horn then began screaming for the car in front of him to move. He nudged the squad car forward until the bars touched the rear bumper of the people mover. The driver got the message and began to pull off to the left. The male in the front seat climbed out then walked swiftly towards the patrol car.

"Whoa, what the hell are you doing Nick?" Darren yelled.

Nick ignored him.

Standing on the accelerator, he blasted through the still red light towards the police station.

Nick took a corner at speed then drove underneath the barrier arm as it slowly lifted out of the way. Tires squealed as the car skidded around the concrete surface in search of an empty space.

As it screeched to a stop, Nick jumped out leaving Darren behind still hanging onto the overhead grab handle.

Nick took the stairs two at a time then burst through the secure door into the rear of the police station. He headed straight for the Captain's office and burst through the door without knocking.

"I need to take some leave." He blurted.

The Captain looked at him then pointed at the door.

'Next time, knock, and no, you can't." The Captain replied with an annoyed expresion.

"Sir you don't understand. I have to go away for a while." He complained.

The Captain shook his head.

"No. We are too busy." He said finally.

"Sir, there has been a problem at home......"

"Sergeant, don't make me tell you again." The Captain warned.

Nick gave up then turned, walked for the door and slammed it shut behind him. He stomped towards his computer terminal and planted himself in his seat. He had to find a way to tell Rossi that he could not be his insider. It ethically and morally wasn't right. But he always came back to the pictures Rossi had in his possession.

Reluctantly, he clicked the internet explorer and began browsing the net for Emery Blackstone.

The Captain pushed the door open and walked down the narrow isle towards the rear of the building. As he past Nick, he cast a hostile glance towards him but said nothing. Captain Tony was used to his little temper tantrums, had even learned to work around them, but lately he was pushing the boundaries, like a two year old testing the parents, and Tony was beginning to grow more than a little pissed off with him.

The Captain walked up to the liaison's desk and dropped a file folder onto it. It landed in front of Melissa, covering her keyboard. She casually picked it up then laid it neatly on the edge of the desk.

"Can I help you Captain?" She asked in her slender American voice.

The Captain looked down at her, he had been told that he was to co-operate fully with the new operative, which he despised.

"Your case file. There has been a large increase of drugs coming into the country, I've been told you are here to investigate the why, how, and who part of that equation. Now, I have told the brass that we don't need any outside help but they have told me, in no uncertain terms, that if I want to keep my job then I am to co-operate, fully, with the new liaison, that being you. So there is everything we have on what's happening." Tony said, pointing down at the file.

"Thank you Captain." Melissa said as sweetly as she could.

"I'm sure this will make my job so much easier."

Captain Tony turned, stalking back to his office gnashing his teeth.

Nick looked across the squad room at the woman sitting at a make shift desk. No one knew where she came from other than what the Captain had told them; she was here to stop the flow of drugs coming in from overseas. Nick shook his head and smiled to himself.

"Good luck with that." He thought.

It was obvious that Tony hated playing baby sitter and resented being left out of the loop.

According to powers higher up the food chain she was an officer from the United States, but other than that there was no more information. She had only been in the country a few weeks.

Nick gazed at her.

She had honey blonde hair and deep green eyes.

She was tall at six foot, her arms spoke of serious gym time. He had to admit that he was jealous of her professionalism, the way she spoke and acted, her body language showed she was totally committed to her profession.

Melissa looked up from her terminal and caught Nick staring at her; she couldn't place her finger on it but there was something about him that she didn't like. Something gnawed at her.

She shook her head turning her attention back to the screen.

So far, Melissa had not been able to come up with anything solid to sell to her superiors back home, she was here alone.

It was part of her assisgnment, to hunt out a certain cartels' reach that had shifted their focus from America and gone global.

Melissa was from the Drug Enforcement Agency but according to the police force in New Zealand she was from the Miami Police Department, on loan to stop drug trafficking out of Cuba. Her real mission was to infiltrate the cartel at the distribution end.

A difficult task for anyone, especially a tall blonde female.

There had been a lot of activity during the previous months, but there was no discernable increase in flow to America, which made the DEA curious.

If it wasn't coming to America, then where was it going?

So far she had tracked some shipments to New Zealand, but after that the trail dead ended, which frustrated her. Melissa took her job seriously, she was going to do everything she could to destroy their distrubution network and put a major dent in their profit line.

Opening the folder, she casually glanced across the squad room again. Baker was staring at his computer screen.

Melissa took the first page from the file to lay it on the desk in front of her. She looked at it carefully. There were only three lines of text on it and a picture.

The picture was of a male, to Melissa he looked around forty. He had a bandana on his head and a ragged goatee. The picture showed that he belonged to the Hellions motorcycle gang. The short rap list indicated he was the violent type putting him in prison a few times. At the bottom of the list was drug running and manufacture.

The bikers name was printed as Robert Ruse, with the alias Robert Cane.

There was some hand written text on the next page indicating that if they could find him then they might be able to find some answers but at the moment they had no other tangible leads to follow.

Melissa looked at the picture, committing it to memory. It was one of her gifts, being able to remember a face. She placed the page back in the file then placed the folder in the top draw of her desk.

Turning the key, she locked the draw and dropped the key into her pocket.

She was still to be officially assigned a partner, which didn't bother her.

She stood up then pushed her chair under the desk and headed for the Captains office.

"I'm going out for a while." She said as she knocked then opened the door.

"Are you sure that's wise, I could send someone with you to show you around more formally." Tony offered.

Melissa shook her head.

"No it's ok." She replied.

The Captain looked at her.

"Your call." He stated as he dropped his gaze back to the newspaper in front of him.

Melissa pulled the door shut and headed for the front door.

Outside it was five thirty and bumper to bumper traffic.

"No different to Miami." She thought.

Melissa stopped at a crosswalk then touched the button to activate the crossing lights. She waited patiently as cars pushed and queued across the intersection in an effort to get home that little bit earlier.

The traffic lights turned orange then red with traffic stalled in the middle of the road blocking access for others as their lights turned green. Melissa ignored them stepping around the bumpers to head for a small shopping complex on the other side.

She had explored the city when she arrived so knew her way around, mostly.

She was fascinated by the infrastructure being crammed into an area that was obviously far too small for it.

Still the council had made it work even if it wasn't very efficient.

Melissa crested a small rise and continued down the other side to a shopping mall. Once inside she turned right then left then right again into a clothing store, found an empty dressing room, then sat down to wait.

Nick tailed the new girl from a distance. She didn't walk fast which made his job a little easier. He didn't have to follow her far either, she was heading for the mall two hundred meters north east on the opposite side of the road from the station house. He stopped and extracted a phone from the bag on his shoulder then jammed it into his pocket, as if he had some important phone call he was waiting for, which he knew wasn't too far from the truth.

He did this while glancing up and to his side to make sure he hadn't lost her in the end of the day crowd. Nick watched Melissa disappear over a rise then quickly followed her. He caught sight of her as she entered the mall. Nick quickened his pace to catch her; he pushed his way through the crowd catching a glimpse of her turning left down one of the mall's main boulevards.

He picked his way through the crowd but lost sight of her. He thought he saw her enter a clothing shop but after ten minutes of searching he couldn't find her. Nick continued to search in frustration; he wanted to know more about this mystery women; he had a bad feeling about her.

Nick's phone chirped, vibrating in his pocket. He dug it out and looked at the display for a number identification, it was blocked. His shoulders slumped and he considered turning it off or letting it ring through to his voice mail, but knew that would have been a foolish decision; reluctantly he accepted the call and raised it to his ear.

"What are you doing?" Rossi asked.

"Nothing." Baker replied, instantly regretting the answer.

"You were told to research Emery Blackstone, Nick, have you done this?" Rossi asked caustically.

Nick lied. "Yes, I am researching him now."

Rossi sighed then took on a quieter tone.

"Good, we need that information and soon. Oh and Nick, don't let me down."

Nick didn't need to research Emery Blackstone. He had read the reports, he was well aware of whom that man was.

He spelt trouble for John Rossi.

CHAPTER 11

My phone spat out its annoying ringtone and began to vibrate, I glanced at it, the small screen telling me it was midday.

Dan and I were about to begin our surveillance. It would take us over an hour to reach Tauranga. I always saw preparation as a key to success.

I picked up the phone and looked at the screen; the number was blocked. I flipped the screen open then put it to my ear and said nothing.

"Mister Blackstone. Emery Blackstone." An electronic voice stated.

I didn't reply.

"If you are listening Emery, if that really is your name, then I think we should meet again, talk business." I could hear static in the background.

"It seems that your offer was of more interest to my superiors than I first thought. They want to know when we can start business. But there are a number of issues that need to be ironed out first."

I stayed quiet and thought about what I was going to say.

"I am waiting for a response Emery. And you should know that I don't like to be kept waiting."

I bit my tongue in an effort to keep quiet.

"I'll assume your silence means the answer is a yes." Rossi stated finally.

The line went dead before I could reply.

I closed the phone and slipped it into my pocket then looked at Dan.

"Looks like we don't have a choice now." I told him.

The drive took nearly two hours. An accident on the gorge road had blocked the two narrow lanes, we caught the tail end of the jam up. We followed a cattle truck to a passing lane then Dan slammed his foot down hard. He was getting sick of waiting.

The van lurched around a corner; I could see the Armco barrier coming dangerously close.

"Slow down would you; we are no good dead in the river." I said looking down at the swollen brown water snaking its way out of the dense bush.

Dan looked across at me then back at the road as he took a corner too fast. The tires squealed in protest as they were pushed to their limits. I could see he was not going to be told, so I shut up and let him drive.

We covered the rest of the distance to Tauranga in less than average time.

Dan pulled the van to the kerb letting me out onto one of the two main roads running through the city. He flicked the indicator and merged into the traffic. We had discussed that he was to remain within a hundred metres of the club to watch the doors. I wanted to get a better feel of the area before I saw John again.

Carefully, I crossed the road and began to make my way towards The Strand.

I could smell the salt hanging in the air and the dampness on the ground. Even though the sky was grey overhead and threatening to rain there were still people out on the streets.

I rounded the corner of a shop then stopped still.

The intersection was busy; crossing lights buzzed as traffic stormed the other way. I looked down the street and saw the van illegally parked in a loading zone yet again, but at least Dan had a good view of the street.

Slowly I continued down the street. Judder bars built into the road were placed every twenty metres to keep the traffic slow, although some people just ignored them and the damage they did to their vehicles.

I crossed the street moving closer to The Strand, towards a sports store, and then stopped at another intersection. To my left I could see the docks used for commercial fishing charters, boat masts bobbing up and down in the gentle swell.

The light flashed and I crossed the street.

The Rossi bar was around the next corner to my left. Slowly I walked towards it glancing to my right. I could see Dan sitting low in the driver's seat watching the entrance. I walked as casually as I could around the corner towards the bar sitting right in the middle of Spring Street Red Square.

A big man with broad shoulders stood at the entrance, I stepped up to him, he placed a hand on my chest and stopped me.

"You can't come in here." He said in a thick voice.

I slowly looked down at his hand then back up at the face staring down at me. He had tattoos scribbled all over the exposed skin on his face that sloped down and disappeared under his dark shirt. I grabbed his hand and shoved it to the side.

"Get out of my way." I whispered.

"What did you say?" The big man asked, leaning forward.

I grabbed the front of his shirt, balled it in my fist then yanked the man off balance. He fell down the step as I stepped past him. Now we were standing as we were before but in opposite positions. The big man looked up at me, suddenly realising that I was just as big as he was. I bunched my shoulders and shoved him backwards away from the door. He stumbled back into a lady carrying a shopping bag knocking her to the pavement. She yelped and looked up at the man with the tattoos on his face. He was standing over her with an angry expression on his face.

The lady started to scream.

As more and more people came to her assistance, I turned on my heel and disappeared into the club closing the door behind me.

The place was a mess.

It stank of alcohol and sweat.

I walked across the dance floor towards the door hidden in the rear wall of the bar.

It was unlocked when I tried the handle so I shoved it open and continued down the hallway to the very end. I opened the door then stepped into the room as if I owned the place slamming it shut. Slowly I took two steps into the empty room and stopped.

The doors behind and in front of me burst open at the same time. The giant stood stooped in one doorway staring at me with dead grey eyes, then a hand landed on my shoulder and began to squeeze. I turned my head slowly to the side, a look of death on my face.

"You have exactly three seconds to get your hand off me before you lose it." I snarled.

The man with the tattooed face looked up and began to laugh then the giant in the doorway coughed.

"Marty." The giant said in his high pitched voice.

The man behind me stopped laughing and took his hand away swiftly; he then turned and walked for the door closing it behind him. The giant said nothing as he stepped out of the doorway into the small room with me, indicating for me to go first. I stepped forward through the door all the time keeping my eyes locked on his.

The room opened out into another at least three times as large as the previous. It was deceptively large.

It was lavishly lined with ornate paintings and items that looked rare and expensive. I casually looked around the room then settled on John sitting behind a mahogany desk.

"It seems, Mister Blackstone, that you aren't very good at taking orders. Why didn't you just tell the doorman you were here to see me?" John asked.

I didn't reply.

"Mister Blackstone, you are going to have to be a little more co-operative if you expect to do business with me." John told me.

I said nothing.

"Look, Mister Blackstone, either co-operate with me or things will get rather painful for you." John told me.

I eyed the giant standing behind him.

I said nothing but dropped my gaze back to John.

"So you say you can double our profits. How exactly do you plan to do that?" Rossi asked.

"I've already told you that." I replied.

"Yes, but I want to hear it again."

I sighed as I glanced down at the dark carpet.

"I'm not going to tell you again." I told him flatly.

Rossi stood up suddenly.

"If you want to do business in this country, you'll need me. Otherwise you will disappear, permanently." He yelled.

I didn't move.

After he had calmed down and returned to his seat I gave it another thirty seconds before I spoke.

"Your name was told to me as the man I could deal with in New Zealand. You come highly recommended from my associates abroad, but I am beginning to think they may have made a mistake." I told him.

Rossi's eyes widened, then narrowed as he absorbed the information.

"Don't play me for a fool Mister Blackstone; I am not a man you want to turn into an enemy." He warned me.

I was beginning to get frustrated; the conversation was going around in circles. I finally relented.

"Ok what do you want to know?" I asked.

"Who are your contacts overseas?" Rossi asked.

I began shaking my head.

"I can't tell you that, they wish to remain anonymous. All I can tell you is that they can shift twice the amount you can shift in a year." I told him.

Rossi remained unmoved.

"That isn't good enough; if I am to do business with you then I want to know who I am dealing with."

I stayed quiet.

I could see Rossi getting uncomfortable, the room was stuffy and he was agitated.

"It seems to me that you know more than enough about me, John. So I want to know something in return. Are you making the drugs here?" I asked.

John looked at me and ground his teeth together.

"That is none of your concern." He spat.

"Yes it is." I replied calmly.

John stood up abruptly again, pointing his index finger at me as he spoke, I could hear his voice beginning to crack with rage.

"You do not need to know. All you need to know is I can supply what you need, and if you try to screw me on this I will kill you and bury you in a very deep hole."

I began to laugh.

"We make our own supply John, we dont really need your assistance, but we have identified an opportunity here so thats why I was asked to come to you. For some reason, my superiors seem to think that we can help each other. But, I don't think you have any idea who you are dealing with John. These people, the people I am employed by, are not the kind of people you want to push around. Your whole operation could vanish into thin air, just like that." I told him, snapping my fingers for effect.

As silence filled the room, I began to think maybe I had pushed it too far.

Then Rossi relaxed, he sat back in his chair, I could see his face change as he came to a decision.

"Ok. Your cut will be three percent." He said as a final offer.

I didn't really care what he offered me so I took it. We shook on it and I headed for the door. As I opened it Rossi told me.

"Tomorrow afternoon we should have a batch ready for sampling. I will call you with details about where to meet." I turned and nodded then closed the door.

Out on the street, I let the breath go I had been holding during the entire meeting. I stepped through the crowd and saw Dan watching from the van. I lifted my hand slowly as if I was about to adjust my collar then spoke into the tiny microphone.

"Did you get all that?" I asked.

I could see Dan nodding his head.

"Ok I'll meet you at the top of the street." I said as I walked past the van without making eye contact.

If I was being tailed again I wanted to lose them in the crowd.

I made my way towards the top of the street stopping at random intervals to look in shop windows. The scene reflected in the window showed nothing alarming.

No tail.

The van pulled up next to me at the intersection, I climbed in as the lights turned green and we disappeared into the traffic.

John looked across the desk at the giant.

"I get the feeling we are about to make a lot of money, but I dont trust Emery, if he's working for a cartel, it could spell major trouble. How is production?" John asked.

"Good at the moment." The giant replied.

"Can we handle the increase?" John asked.

The giant shook his head.

"What do we need?"

"More labour."

Chapter 12

Amy flicked through a medical journal. She had read some interesting articles on a revolutionary new drug that had claimed to stop cancer cells in its tracks. Amy scoffed, she knew all about cancer cells and their ability to adapt.

She turned to the rear pages where they had advertisements for careers and jobs listings. She skimmed through the usual job listings for doctors wanted in small rural towns or hospitals.

Amy ignored these.

Instead she browsed the ads for pharmaceutical companies. One ad caught her attention. It asked her if she wanted to travel, if she liked to work in exotic places, if she wanted to make a difference.

Amy read the remainder of the ad then looked at the number. It was a New Zealand number.

She removed her cell phone from her bag and tapped the number into the key pad.

"Signature Pharmaceuticals, how may I direct your call?" A pleasant voice asked.

"Yes, I am ringing about the job in the Medical Times."

"I'm sorry but that position has been filled." The polite voice told her.

Amy's shoulders slumped.

She stayed quiet as the lady clicked keys on her keyboard.

"But it seems that we have just had another brought to our attention. It is similar in scope and is located in Auckland, New Zealand." The voice told her.

Amy bit her lip.

"Do you know if they are they recruiting students?" Anticipation heavy in her voice.

She heard fingers tapping keys on a keyboard.

"Yes, they are." The voice stated after a moment.

Amy couldn't believe her luck, she asked for some contact details, wrote them down on her text book, then hung up the phone. She looked at the number she had written down and began to wonder what it would entail.

She carefully pushed the numbers into the phone then hit send. The phone clicked once then began to ring. It was answered after the fourth ring.

"Yes?." A deep male voice asked.

"Yes, hello, I'm calling about the job that was advertised by Signature Pharmaceuticals, well not really advertised by them but they told..."

"I know the opportunity you are talking about. We haven't filled it yet." The voice told her cutting her off.

Amy felt her heart skip a beat.

If she could land a high paying job before she was finished at university, she knew she would be the envy of everyone in her class.

"Would you like to apply for it?" The man's voice asked.

She caught herself nodding halfway through the question and answered affirmatively, just as the man finished the question.

"Well then, we had better get some details from you." The voice stated.

Amy couldn't contain her excitement as she rattled off every phone number where they could get in touch with her, told them where she lived and what she was studying at university.

The male voice told her they would be in touch with the employment opportunity details.

She put the journal down on the park bench in front of her then gazed around the campus.

Karen was due to finish her class soon, Amy debated with herself if she should tell her. She glanced at her watch as Karen sat down next to her.

"Guess what." Amy blurted.

Karen leaned back with a surprised expression.

"I've landed a job." Amy told her, unable to control herself.

Karen looked at her. Eyes wide.

"What do you mean 'job'. You haven't finished yet." Karen told her.

The smile on Amy's face vanished.

"Thanks for your support." She pouted.

"Sorry... I mean what about your degree, you have to finish that to even be looked at." Karen told her.

Amy nodded.

"I guess I'll have to work that into the contract." She told Karen.

Karen looked at her, began shaking her head as a smile grew across her lips.

"You're unbelievable. Why do these kinds of things always land in your lap?" Karen asked in mock frustration.

Amy just shrugged her shoulders.

"Don't know. Gifted I guess."

Karen rolled her eyes.

"Dream on darling."

The pair stood up then began walking towards the edge of the campus and back towards their small apartment in the city.

John's phone chirped, he looked at the display. It was a number he knew all too well, the tune filling his office at the port of Tauranga. He picked it up and looked harder at the number hoping he had misread it, he hadn't.

"Yes sir." He answered after he flipped the screen back.

To anyone listening, be it nearby or with electronic devices, they would have only heard a string of letters and numbers.

John quickly grabbed a pad then began scribbling down the sequence, all the time hoping he hadn't and wouldn't miss a number or letter. If he did, it could spell big trouble for him. Trouble that could get him killed.

The sequence had proven to be fool proof, it was proported to be unbreakable and meant nothing if the message happened to be intercepted by the authorities. The only way it could be deciphered was with the key.

And that was changed every thirty six hours.

The sequence stopped and the connection was severed. John knew from experience that there would be an encrypted email with the latest version of the key in his inbox soon.

He closed his phone and dropped it on his desk, then looked outside towards the mountain at the end of the beach, sitting like a guardian to the entrance of the harbour.

A knock at the door startled him; he spun around in his chair quickly regaining his composure before he answered.

"What?" He barked.

The giant pushed the door open then stepped forward one step, turned and slammed it shut. The giant was wearing dark glasses and a suit that was tailored to his large dimensions, even though, it still looked ridiculously tight on him.

The giant walked forward two paces to stand exactly in the centre of John's office.

His large head cranked forward and looked down at John. John knew what was coming, he tried to sink back in his chair.

The giant removed his glasses and looked at him with hard grey eyes.

"I don't like this new player." The giant stated in a high voice.

"And I don't like what you are doing." The giant said, pointing a large finger at him.

"You are risking too much for little benefit, for something you don't even know this guy can deliver." The giant stated.

John knew even though he looked stupid, the truth was the giant was anything but.

"We have been through this already." John sighed hoping to regain some control.

The giant looked down at the floor of the office. It was carpeted in plush red wool.

"If this comes back." The giant said as he leaned on the desk. "You will get us both killed."

John swallowed hard and hoped the giant didn't notice it. He stood up slowly then walked around to the edge of the desk and looked down on the port below. Three big ships were docked against the wharf. Container cranes mounted on the edge of the docks were slowly unloading containers onto the wharf where large forklifts would take them to their designated area for devanning.

John could almost picture their boat arriving at the port. Even though it was a small operation, it was a critical part of the process. It would be dwarfed by the boats around it but John estimated that it would be worth at least one hundred times the value of any container vessel along side it. He knew it would never get there though, the risk would be too great.

If the authorities flaged the boat for inspection, his entire end of the operation could collapse. Not only for the flow into New Zealand but also the flow back to the United States.

John turned, walked back to his desk and looked down at the piece of paper with the undeciphered code written on it. He picked it up to study it more closely; he had received these types of transmissions before and noted that it was longer than usual. He wasn't bothered though, it would be an instruction about their new business partner.

"This won't come back on us. They've already told me to handle it, so that is what I'm doing." He told the giant.

The giant gazed at him for a second too long then turned for the door. He paused with his hand resting on the handle.

"In the interest of keeping this operation a viable business we need to find out what this new player wants." The giant stated to John without turning around.

John nodded but stayed silent. The giant swung the door open then disappeared down the short hallway to the dock below.

CHAPTER 13

Martin Wong was a biker, he was five foot six and heavily tattooed. He loved his motorcycle more than anything that had ever entered his life. It was his and his alone, no one was going to touch or take his pride and joy. He pulled into the small driveway at his gang head quarters in Glenview, Hamilton. The driveway was specifically designed narrow so the police could not drive their cars up to the front door. It had been Martin's idea which had prompted the gang leader to appoint him head of security, which was ironic, before he became a patched member and covered in ink, he was involved with a security firm that catered to the major banks within New Zealand.

Martin had morals though.

Even so, the leaders of the gang had tried to persuade him to break into a bank in another city. They thought because that he knew where the sensors and cameras would be located and how to disable the alarm systems, that the robbery would be a breeze. Martin tried to persuade them to the contrary but they would not listen.

All they could see was easy money.

He knew it would be a bad idea and he showed them exactly what he meant.

The leaders devised a plan to send in a group of prospects, their instructions were to empty the tellers terminals, then the vault. Martin ran them through the procedures until they became agitated at the constant instructions and told him to get lost. He tried to make them listen but they didn't want to hear another word.

The heist was a complete failure.

The leaders, along with Martin, watched from a distance as the crew entered the bank. They created chaos and confusion rather quickly which was according to plan until one of the prospects jumped the gun and started grabbing handfuls of money from an open till before the alarms could be deactivated.

The police had arrived in a matter of minutes.

Martin turned to the leaders and tried to again explain what enevitably happened.

The gang leaders turned away saying nothing.

Martin pulled his cut down Harley around the corner of the house and parked it on a hard stand that had been laid specifically for the members' bikes.

The prospects had to park on the street.

He killed the ignition then reached down under the tank and pressed a small button arming a kill device that activated after ten seconds if the engine was hot wired. Martin was quite proud of it, the design was his own, he had managed to sell a few hundred units to people he knew. He even converted them for use in cars.

The unit wasn't strictly legal but it did an effective job.

Martin climbed the steps to the back door and pushed it open.

The house smelt strongly of marijuana and alcohol. Martin detested illegal drugs and refused to touch them. He drank and smoked tobacco, but would not be given dope.

He stalked down a narrow hallway towards the centre of the house. A large banner ran the length of the hall towards the centre of the house baring the gang's name and insignia. Martin ignored it and kept walking. He shoved the door open and stepped into a large living area. In the centre was a large low coffee table with seats positioned all around it, against the outer walls of the room were more seats to accommodate more people.

Martin walked across the stained carpet; he looked down to study a few spots before he stepped on them then addressed the gang leader.

"You called?" Martin asked.

The gang leader looked up at his head of security, eyeing him through a thick veil of smoke.

"You have a job to do." The leader told him.

Martin nodded sagely.

"And what job is that?" He asked.

The president leaned forward placing a fat joint on the edge of an ash tray then stood up.

At six foot six and three hundred pounds, he was a formidable sight and very few people dared to mess with him. The gang leader stuffed an oversize hand into his filthy jeans pocket and removed a small photograph then handed it to Martin.

"None of these other idiots here are capable of pulling this off. If you come through then we stand to make a substantial amount of cash. If you do not…well." The gang leader just shrugged his shoulders.

Martin knew what that meant. If he failed, his body would probably be found in a years time at the bottom of some natural hole in the middle of the dense bush along the east coast. Martin knew failure was not tolerated.

He lifted the photo and studied it carefully. The person in the photo looked ordinary enough but Martin had not survived this long by being stupid. He knew appearances could be deceiving.

Martin looked at the leader.

"What has this person done?" He asked.

"Nothing. All you need to do is bring them back here." The leader stated.

Martin nodded then turned and walked for the exit. He didn't need to ask any more questions, he knew the information from his own people would be unreliable at best, he would therefore have to glean his own.

Martin climbed aboard his bike and pointed it north towards Auckland. He knew the best place to start looking was the big city.

Chapter 14

Dan sat on the porch of his low lying villa and gazed out over the short three hundred metre range he had fashioned out of the terrain that was his property. The back stop was a hundred and fifty foot tall hillside that offered ample protection to anything beyond it.

Next to him on a specially designed shooting bench, rested a Savage model 12FVSS on a bi-pod, a bolt action rifle chambered in 5.56 NATO. Mounted on a picatinny rail was a Leupold Mark 4 varipower scope. The magnification could be wound from six and a half times right up to twenty four making it ideal for long distance shooting. A suppressor almost three inches in diameter was screwed to the muzzle. It was manufactured by a gunsmith that lived half an hour south of him. The man said it would reduce the noise signature of the NATO round to nothing more than that of an air rifle.

Three hundred metres was hardly a stretch for this particular combination of rifle and scope so Dan had made it a little more interesting.

Ping pong balls were tied to lengths of string hanging almost a metre from the ground on a metal frame. The range ran north to south making the prevailing easterly breeze a simple trigonometry calculation for a fixed target; what made the targets difficult was the breeze; they floated from side to side, sometimes by up to a metre. Dan cradled a set of binoculars in his hands and watched the breeze gently sway the soft grass towards the target area. He judged it to be moving around five kilometres an hour, not normally a difficult shot with a larger calibre but the smaller sixty three grain projectile is a lot more susceptible to wind.

Dan placed the binoculars on the bench then tucked himself down behind the rifle. He positioned his elbows as comfortable as he could then gently pushed the bolt forward stripping a round from the magazine locking it into the chamber.

He watched the small plastic balls dance in the breeze three hundred metres away. Dan settled on the centre target; his breathing calm and heart beating slowly.

The ball moved left to right in front of the cross hairs, Dan timed the breeze watching the ball carefully. The target found a lull in the breeze swaying only minutely with the tiny air currents around it.

Dan's index finger squeezed the trigger slowly but surely, the rifle coughed. The small ball three hundred metres away flicked upwards as it shattered. The projectile hit the target square on removing it from the metal frame.

Dan breathed in then out slowly. He smiled to himself then lifted the bolt handle and extracted the case. He caught it as it sprung from the bolt face.

"Excellent shot. Remind me never to get on your bad side." A voice said to him.

Dan had become so engrossed in the target that he failed to hear a car pull up behind him. He sat up then turned and gazed up at the figure backlit by the afternoon sun. The man was dressed in a suit and black formal dress shoes.

He glanced at the silver BMW parked behind his old van then back up at the person.

Dan stood up and the sun disappeared revealing the person to him. It was a face he hadn't seen in years. It was a face he was hoping he would never have to see again. The man stepped forward offering his hand.

Dan didn't take it.

"Dan, it's good to see you again." The man said as a smile crept across his face.

Dan said nothing.

"Come on, I come all this way and not even a hand shake for your long lost relative?" The man asked.

Dan said nothing.

The man shrugged his shoulders.

"Ok. I know you aren't happy to see me, I get that… then what are you doing here?" Dan asked cutting him off.

The man gazed down range to watch the small white dots swaying in the breeze before he answered.

"I've turned over a new leaf." The man stated.

Dan grinned and dropped his head not believing a word he was saying or about to say.

"As you can see now I've made something of myself." The man indicated to the BMW.

Dan looked over his shoulder saying nothing, waiting for him to elaborate.

"I'm a private investigator now." The man said as he removed a card from a hidden jacket pocket then extended it towards Dan with trained precision.

Dan looked up at his relation and laughed.

"You, an investigator!"

He watched the man's eyes narrow in anger.

Dan stepped forward abruptly meeting his relative toe to toe knocking the card to the ground.

"I don't believe you." Dan whispered, all traces of humour gone from his voice.

The man's eyes darted from left to right unwilling to meet Dan's. Eventually the man stepped back.

"Believe what you want, this is what I do now, and I was told you would be able to help me." Dan began to shake his head.

"Why the hell would I want to help you?" He asked caustically.

"I'm trying to find someone. The people who hired me think she is in danger. She hasn't been in touch with anyone from her family for at least a year and has virtually disappeared."

Dan looked at the man and said nothing.

"Her locations are random at best, but at least she is still in the country. Right?"

Dan looked down at the ground and began to shake his head again.

"Idiot." He muttered.

"Pardon me?" The man asked.

Dan shook his head and kept his gaze on the ground.

"I can't help you." Dan stated finally looking up.

"Can't or won't?" The man asked.

"Won't."

"I see." Said the man.

"Oh well, don't be surprised if she turns up raped or dead." The man carried on.

Dan turned and looked down the range. He was getting close to about all he could stomach of this man.

"I think it's time for you to leave." Dan told him flatly.

The man put his hands up as if surrendering, slowly a grin formed across his lips. He had pushed him too far, exactly as he had planned.

"Ok, ok, take it easy, sport. Just thought you might have an ear to the ground or know something. That was all." The man slowly lowered his hands.

Dan said nothing.

The man slowly backed away towards the car then turned halfway, dropping his hands to his side.

Dan stood still and watched the car move down the driveway all the way to the road then vanish over a small rise before he turned back to the range. He stopped midstride and thought about what his scum of a relative had just told him.

Was he really a P.I.?

Was he really trying to turn over a new leaf?

Dan shook his head and knew he wasn't, he corrected himself and said 'could not'.

The man was too involved in crime. If Dan had to guess he would have wagered money on the BMW being stolen.

He turned slightly then walked back to his house. Inside he reached for his phone and dialled Emery's number. Emery picked up on the second ring.

"We may have a problem." Dan stated.

"Uh huh, and what would that be?" The electronic voice asked.

He ran through the details of the impromptu meeting with his long lost relative while Emery remained silent. Emery knew all too well about people who said they had turned over a new leaf.

"All I can suggest is that you find this person before he does. If what you say is true then she may be in trouble." The electronic voice told Dan.

"Ok." He replied.

He promised to keep Emery updated before he hung up the phone.

Dan stepped back outside into the darkening twilight and looked down at the gravel driveway. The card was still where it had landed. Dan walked over, picked the card up then turned it over. It showed a name which was fake, and a cell phone number.

He slipped the card into his pocket, collected the rifle and the remainder of his gear then walked back to the house. Fifteen minutes later he was on the road and heading south. He knew better than to place a call from his house. If someone was listening he wanted to be somewhere else.

CHAPTER 15

Melissa walked down the darkened street. She lived close by and the walk home helped clear her thoughts, allowing her to decompress. She had finished her shift for the day but was still on the clock according to the DEA. The darkness between the overhead streetlights swallowed her up. She glanced over her shoulder to confirm the feeling that had gnawed at her since she left the station house. A shadowy figure moved quickly behind a tree about fifty metres behind her. Similar dealings in her home country had made her ready for any eventuality, if it came down to it, she was prepared to do whatever was necessary.

Dan reached the small town of Te Awamutu. He pulled tight to the curb next to a pay phone and climbed out of the van. He dialled the number on the card and the phone answered on the third ring.

"What?" A man's voice asked.

Dan clenched his teeth but kept his voice calm.

"You want my help?" Dan answered.

"Dan, yes I do." The man replied, this time much more friendly.

Dan resisted the urge to slam the phone down.

"What do you want then?"

Dan heard the man shuffling around in the background.

"I have a photo of the person I'm trying to find. Is there some way I can get it to you."

Dan thought quickly then gave him Emery's secure line. It couldn't be traced.

"Ok, I'll send it through now. Is that where you are now?" The man asked.

Dan ignored the question.

"If this is some sort of scheme you've planned to cook me with, think again." Dan slammed the phone down.

Even though the guy was family he couldn't stand talking to him.

Dan climbed into his van, pointing it north. It would take him roughly an hour to reach Emery's but he knew that he would be in touch before then.

Dan's phone chirped twenty minutes later.

"Why am I looking at a faxed photo of a twenty something year old girl?" Emery asked.

"She's the person my P.I conartist relation is trying to find. I haven't seen it." Dan said as he navigated through Hamilton city.

"Ok, so where are we going to start?" Emery asked.

"Where we usually start, police database. I'll be at yours in about forty minutes." Dan said then hung up the phone.

I placed the photo and the phone on the table. I gazed at the photo, the smiling face looking back at me. Eventually I looked away.

The aroma of chicken curry floated through the house as Dan showed up forty minutes later.

"She certainly doesn't look like the type to go missing." Dan said as he picked the photo off the table.

I looked at him as I stabbed my last piece of chicken.

"I didn't know people had a look to go missing." Dan turned the photo to me again.

"She's smiling. By the looks of it there was an arm around her shoulder when this was taken so one could assume she had at least one friend. I mean her general appearance looks like someone who is happy with life, not someone who would just up and disappear."

I chewed on the piece of chicken while I thought about it.

He was right.

She looked like the wrong type of person to go missing.

"Get into the database and see what you can dig up." I said pointing to the computer.

Dan looked at it then walked over to deposit himself into the leather seat at the keyboard. He touched the mouse causing the screen to redraw into my screen saver.

The business end of my custom built target rifle.

He clicked the internet explorer icon which brought up the Google home page. It didn't take him long, he was past the firewall and into the police intranet.

His first port of call was the missing persons list. In total it had thirty names and faces but none looked like the grainy image in the photo.

I sat down at the table to watch him scroll the photos at a blurry speed. He clicked on a few but none looked even remotely close. I studied the photo closely. She had blonde hair and dark eyes. She looked fit and healthy, her eyes weren't sunken and her face wasn't gaunt.

Something didn't add up.

"I don't think you are going to find her under missing persons." I said as I placed the photo in front of me.

Dan nodded then grabbed the photo from the table. He placed it under the scanner cover then started a program that would copy the image to a file. The grainy image popped up in front of him, I watched intently as he manipulated the program in ways I didn't even know were possible. It took him close to fifteen minutes before he had the image as close to perfect as he could get.

Dan saved the image under a file name then opened his program called *'HideandSeek'* that uses facial recognition software. He loaded the file into the program then opened the drivers licence data base and hit the start button.

The program was designed to search for information by matching facial features. He told me it was at least ninety percent accurate but it took a while to scroll through everything.

Dan stood up, shoved the chair back then walked to the kitchen. I watched the computer as it clicked and whirred not really doing anything.

"Where's your coffee." He asked from the kitchen.

"Bottom shelf." I called back.

I heard a cup thump on the kitchen counter then the clatter of a spoon as a scoop of coffee was dropped into the cup. The fridge opened then slammed shut with a kick, I kept looking at the computer.

It stopped clicking and whirring then slowly let a picture draw on the screen.

"Got something." I called to him as the jug began to boil.

"That was fast. Usually takes longer." Dan called back.

He lifted the jug and poured boiling water into the coffee then gave the mix a quick stir.

I sat at the table smelling the aroma of coffee wafting through from the kitchen while slowly reading the information on the screen.

Dan placed the dangerously full cup on the desk and pulled the chair in close to the keyboard.

"Amy Tarrant. Lives in Auckland, surprise, surprise."

"Ok, what else can you find on her?" I asked.

Dan saved the information to the photo file then opened the internet explorer. He typed the name into the search engine and hit enter.

Two names appeared. One was a prostitute, the other was a medical student. Dan moved the cursor and clicked on the med student.

The screen redrew into the Auckland University website and directed us towards medical studies.

It told us Amy was a med student majoring in chemistry. She was in a class of twenty students and into her third year. It didn't say anything about a home address, which was good, but it would be easy enough to find.

Dan pulled a small cell phone from his pocket then flipped the screen open; he hesitated and slapped it shut again.

"What?" I asked.

"My relation. I know I can't trust him." He replied.

"Then don't tell him. We'll go find Amy and bring her back to where ever she was from."

As I said the words something didn't ring right.

Dan turned and looked at me.

Chapter 16

Amy lay in bed.

It was late, she could hear Karen through the wall in the next room, snoring, again.

She pulled the pillow over her head and tried to go to sleep. After fifteen minutes her head became hot and sweaty and she found it hard to breathe.

On the plus side though her flatmate's snoring had been temporarily drowned out. Slowly she pulled the pillow away, to her delight the noise had vanished.

Amy flipped the pillow over so the cooler side was facing up then pulled the covers up around her neck. She was on her side lying with her back to the door.

Slowly, her eyes drooped shut and a tiny smile spread over her lips.

As Amy settled she heard one of the floor boards creak, her eyes flicked open.

'Karen must be up getting a glass of water'. She thought to herself.

A massive hand clamped over Amy's mouth and nose then another snaked around her neck.

The stench of halothane clogged her nostrils and choked her.

Amy struggled and fought, trying to scream but she couldn't move. Slowly she could feel her limbs cease to scramble, with each second her muscles began to fade. The last thing she remembered was asking herself, *'why me?'*

Martin slowly removed his hands from around Amy's slender throat and mouth.

He stood up then wiped his hands on his jeans. He could still feel the other girl's blood on his skin sticking his fingers together; they were becoming slippery as the blood dried.

The knife across her throat had been a fast and effective way of making sure she wouldn't become a problem.

Martin turned in the darkness as he went to stuff the halothane soaked rag into his pocket but it slipped from his grip. He cursed and bent down groping the floor to find it. After a minute of desperate searching in the dark he gave up, he didn't think it was a big deal anyway.

Amy had struggled as he had hoped, making the halothane enter her blood stream all that much faster. He rolled her over on to her stomach then laced her wrists together with two zip ties.

Next, Martin took a small but wide roll of masking tape from a pocket in his jacket and wrapped it half a dozen times around her mouth being careful not to block her nose; she was no good to anyone dead.

Carefully, he lifted her small body from the bed and cradled her in his arms then silently made his way for the back door of the building.

He didn't want to be too long on site. He knew he was reasonably safe but if some passerby saw him it could spell a lot of trouble.

Martin loaded Amy's inert body into the back of a van in near total darkness. All that lay on the back floor was a blanket and a bottle of water as was instructed. Martin closed the door quietly then quickly made his way to the driver's seat. The van fired and settled into a low rumble then slowly pulled out onto a side street. He made his way to the motorway then turned the van south. By the time he drove past the Bombay Service Centre at the speed limit the time was close to midnight.

Chapter 17

I arrived at Dan's place at a quarter to seven, almost an hour early because I couldn't sleep. I kept turning the situation about Amy over in my head, something just didn't add up. Quietly I made my way to the front door and knocked against it three times. A lady answered the door. She had a shock of bright pink hair that draped just past her shoulder blades. She wore a thin white flannelette shirt that was ten times too large for her slender frame, her feet bare, it looked like that was all she had time to put on before she let me in.

"You're after Dan aren't you?" She asked still half asleep.

I nodded.

I stood still in the doorway waiting to be invited in as she turned then walked back into the living room. She turned back and looked at me.

"You can come in." She told me.

I kicked my boots off, slipped inside then closed the door behind me. I took two steps and leaned against the counter top that separated the small kitchen from the living room. The lady clicked the kettle on and pulled three cups from a cupboard beneath the sink. She placed them on the bench then turned to look at me.

"I'm Roxy. Tea or coffee?" She asked.

I looked towards the hallway as a door slammed shut and another opened then back at Roxy.

"Tea, please, herbal if you have it." I answered.

Roxy nodded and extracted a bag of some herbal tea from the same cupboard as the cups. She dropped it in the cup then poured hot water over it.

Steam drifted off the cup and rose towards the ceiling. She picked it up and placed it on the counter in front of me without saying another word.

I figured she wasn't a morning person.

Dan walked out of the hallway buttoning a shirt. He looked at my cup then at Roxy's cup on the bench. I picked up my cup and went to stand on the deck.

Dan stepped outside and pushed his feet into his shoes.

"She didn't make me a cup of tea." He stated solemnly.

I turned to look at him.

"Are you two going to have a domestic, I can leave if you like?" I told him, not knowing whether he was serious or not.

Dan burst out laughing as Roxy stepped through the door with a coffee cup.

"What's so funny?" She asked.

Dan shook his head as he turned and accepted the cup from his wife.

Roxy shrugged then went back inside.

I said nothing as I sipped the bitter tea while listening to the early morning sounds. The air was cool and crisp.

"Should be a nice day." Dan stated looking up at the early morning cloudless sky.

I nodded and said nothing.

"So, what are we going to do when we find Amy?" Dan asked.

I shrugged my shoulders and said nothing.

It was another five minutes before either of us spoke again.

"What if she's gone?" He asked.

"Well, then, I suppose we shall have a word with your relative." I told him.

Dan nodded and smiled.

I had a feeling there was some unfinished business between Dan and the mysterious relative who happened to be a private investigator.

The drive towards Auckland was slow. An accident at the on ramp at Bombay had morning commuter traffic backed up to the other side of the hill. We managed to snake our way through the tangled mess.

A car had clipped the side of a fuel tanker and rolled in the north bound lane. It cleared the median barrier, coming to rest in the centre of the south bound lanes jamming traffic in both directions.

Dan whistled.

"I didn't think there were that many cars on the road during the morning."

I watched the line of traffic stretch at a stand still half way down the Runciman straight. Up in the distance by the Drury turnoff I could see flashing lights spread out over the road screaming towards us in the south bound lanes.

"That's going to be busy for a while." I stated as I turned back to the front.

Dan nodded but said nothing.

We reached the address Dan had found online for Amy. It was a quiet suburban back street in Morningside.

Dan turned left down the tight street and bumped over a judder bar. We drove halfway down the tarseal then pulled up to the address.

I looked up the short path to the front door.

It was closed.

I was beginning to think this was a wild chase.

But still.

"Wait here." I said as I climbed out of the passenger side.

I pushed the door closed quietly, probably more than was strictly necessary for an urban street but old habits die hard.

I made my way across the foot path to the small metal gate that entered the property.

It hung open.

Following the path up towards the front door, an eerie quietness settled around me, sending a shiver up my spine. Blossom trees covered the front lawn obscuring my view of the front windows. I reached the front door and gently rapped on the solid wood.

No answer.

I tried again, this time a bit louder.

Still no answer.

I had walked up a small step onto a landing so I turned around then dropped to a crouch to look under the trees towards Dan. I shook my head and pointed to the rear of the house. He nodded and began to open his door.

I stood up then began quietly walking around the garden towards the rear.

All the windows were closed and the curtains were drawn. Not surprising I thought, especially as Amy is a student.

Maybe her classes didn't start until later on in the day.

As I approached the back of the house, I saw the rear door hanging open by the slightest margin and was suddenly hit with a sickening feeling.

I raced for the door then stopped.

It had been forced open.

I took a handkerchief from my pocket and gently pushed the door open. It let me into the kitchen.

The space looked lived in; people had been here not too long ago. The sink had a couple days worth of dishes stacked in it but the rest looked clean and tidy. I moved slowly through the kitchen towards the centre of the house.

The living room was joined to the kitchen but separated by the counter top partitioning it off from the rest of the room. Against the far wall sat a huge television. It was surrounded by a large black leather sofa with two smaller double chairs either side, between them was a small low coffee table.

The floor was wooden but covered in rugs of assorted colours. I ignored it all and turned towards the short hallway that ran down the centre of the house then started towards it.

"What have you found?" Dan whispered.

His voice caught me off guard and startled me but I didn't show it.

"Nothing, yet."

I carried on towards the entrance to the hallway and slowly made my way towards the rooms. There were five doors to choose from.

One I guessed was the linen cupboard.

I reached for the first handle and swung the door open.

It was empty except for a computer on a desk surrounded by a mess of papers.

I stepped into the room then read some of the letters.

'Power bills, phone bills." I stated for Dan.

Something else caught my eye. It was a note pad; on the top page was a string of equations that looked like a foreign language. I pointed to it, Dan looked down.

"Looks like chemistry of some description."

I glanced around the room then headed for the door.

"Let's check the rest of the house."

In the next room we found what I hoped we wouldn't.

A dead girl.

She looked like she had been murdered where she lay. Her throat had been sliced from one side of her neck to the other. Blood had pooled beneath her staining the sheets a dark red, contrasting dramatically with the original white.

I shook my head and felt my anger rise.

We checked the next room and found an empty bed which looked like it had been vacated in a hurry. Like that person had woken abruptly and rushed to stand up.

I bent down to look under the bed and saw nothing. It wasn't until I turned to the left and looked under the night stand that I saw it.

A rag. A dirty coloured rag.

I carefully picked it up and studied it.

"Take a look at this." I called to him.

Dan stepped over and looked at it.

"What?" He asked confused.

I looked at him.

"This, it doesn't fit." I told him.

His confusion stayed firmly in place.

"The rest of the house is clean and tidy then you have this, under the night stand." I said, pointing down at the floor. Dan nodded.

"Dropped by the killer." He said as a statement.

I lifted the rag so I could take a closer look at it.

Dan leaned in.

"You smell that?" I asked.

"Ether." Dan replied.

"Or something similar."

I carried the rag out to the car through the back door again being careful not to touch anything on the way.

As we moved off down the street, I carefully placed the rag in a plastic bag and zipped the top shut. Dan pulled over beside a payphone and I climbed out. My collar came up and I kept my face looking at the ground as I dialled triple one.

"Police." I told the operator.

Once the police operator came on the line I told them what they needed to hear then hung up. Quickly I returned to the car then pulled the door shut.

"Now we go and have a talk to my relative." Dan stated.

I nodded and we turned to head south.

Chapter 18

Melissa pushed the door open to the station house and stepped inside. It was a lot warmer inside than out. Melissa stripped off her heavy coat and scarf then draped them over the back of her chair. Captain Tony made a bee line straight for her desk.

"You and Nick are together today. There's a homicide, here is the address." He stated as he handed her a slip of paper.

Melissa looked across the desk at Nick who was listening to the conversation unfold. Melissa read the address then looked back across at Nick. She still couldn't figure him out, yet, but she knew he was no good.

"You drive?" She asked.

Nick just nodded then stood and grabbed his coat from the back of his seat.

The traffic was heavy. It was a Monday morning.

There had been a crash on the Bombay Hills that had congested it in both directions.

Nick drove in silence but every now and then he stole glances at Melissa. She could see him out of the corner of her eye but ignored him; she was too busy thinking about the shadow that had been following her home.

Nick found a gap in the traffic and pushed the squad car down the motorway at an excessive speed, Melissa glanced across at him.

"Are we late for something?" She asked casually.

"Huh?" Nick grunted.

Melissa pointed down at the speedo. The needle was bouncing off one hundred and forty kilometres per hour. Nick looked down, his eyes widened. He took his foot of the gas to slow the car down to the posted speed limit. Melissa turned to him to ask a question but thought better of it.

Nick drove down Dominion road dead on the speed limit. He hit the lights at the intersection of Balmoral and Dominion then swung the wheel left. They drove for five hundred metres then turned right onto Sandringham road and drove towards the scene. It was another five hundred metres until he pulled left onto Leslie Avenue and slowed to a halt behind two squad cars.

Nick climbed out of the car without a word then slammed the door. He marched towards the house and the officer standing at the front door. He stepped up to the uniform flashing his badge. The officer looked at the badge then at him. Nick went to step through the door but the officer blocked his way momentarily. Nick glared at him.

"Good morning officer." Melissa said to the man at the door.

The officer looked past Nick and nodded at her.

"Ma'am."

Nick spun around surprised to see Melissa standing behind him and cursed himself for not hearing her approach. He turned back to the officer glaring at him some more.

He was about to tell the officer who exactly was in charge when Melissa cut him off.

"We're here to investigate the homicide." She told the officer in her sweet American voice.

The officer nodded then moved aside and opened the door for them; he ignored Nick but nodded again to Melissa as she stepped over the threshold.

Nick said nothing as he stalked through the living room; he ignored Melissa and the surroundings completely. He wanted to see the bodies. He stepped into the hallway and saw another officer looking into a room. Nick cleared his throat as he approached, to his delight it had the desired effect, the officer stepped away from the room then cranked his head to see who was approaching. When he saw it was Nick, the officer visibly stiffened. Nick stepped past him, into the bedroom and fixed his eyes on the bloody mess.

"How much of the crime scene have you contaminated?" Nick asked the officer without taking his eyes off the girl.

"Ah…..um, nothing." The officer stuttered.

Nick spun around and stared at him, ice in his eyes.

"You were told to wait for a homicide detective, but you couldn't help yourself, your curiosity got the better of you, you had to stick you nose in and contaminate what evidence might be available to us to catch the killer." Nick whispered with a lethal undertone.

The cop balked then stepped backwards into the hallway nearly bumping into Melissa; he spun around to see her looking from him to Nick. Nick turned away with a disgusted look on his face.

Melissa indicated for the cop to leave but Nick stopped him.

Without turning around he asked. "Where is the other body?"

The cop looked at the back of Nick's head then at Melissa.

"There's only one body." He replied.

Melissa screwed her nose up as she looked at Nick who still hadn't turned around.

The uniform brushed past Melissa in the narrow hallway and disappeared into the living room.

Melissa stepped into the room to stand beside Nick.

"Nobody said anything about another body Nick, what aren't you telling me?" She asked.

Nick turned and stepped abruptly towards her then stopped. Melissa was waiting for him to say something, the muscles in his jaw twitching. She could read the anger in his face.

"You know as much as I do." He told her, his words clipped.

He stepped past her and into the hallway disappearing from view.

Chapter 19

Amy awoke to pitch black.

Her temples throbbed, she groaned as she tried to lift her head.

Then panic hit her.

Memories began flooding back, the hand across her mouth, the sickening smell of the rag.

And the hand across her throat.

She remembered the hand across her throat, she touched it involuntarily.

She could feel a bruise forming.

Amy sat up and opened her eyes.

Bolts of pain ripped through her temples, she felt herself waver as spots danced in front of her.

Amy forced herself to breathe and concentrate on relaxing the muscles around her neck. It worked, the pain began to subside slowly, very slowly.

Opening her eyes again, she looked around but found there was no light, it was absolutely pitch black. Amy opened her eyes wide until she could feel the pain beginning to increase again but was rewarded with only darkness.

She tried to stand up.

As soon as she reached her feet she knew she had made a mistake. Light spots exploded all around her, blinding her, sending shards of crippling pain through her head. This time she felt her knees weaken, her head swung forward as she reached out in front of her to arrest her fall but found nothing.

Amy crashed to the floor surrounded by darkness.

Martin Wong pulled into the driveway to the gang pad a week later. He parked his bike on the hard stand at the rear of the headquarters then walked up the concrete steps to the door. As he pushed it open, he thought about what he was going to tell the president.

Then the sickening smell of drugs hit him as he stepped across the threshold.

He reached the living room and took in the surroundings; he thought it looked like it had deteriorated somewhat in the week he wasn't there.

The leader stepped out of a side room blowing a huge cloud of blue smoke towards the centre of the living room.

"I hear good news." The large man stated, as if he already knew Martin had completed the job successfully.

Martin stayed quiet waiting for him to elaborate.

"Where have you taken her?" The leader asked.

Martin looked down at the stained carpet, he chose his words carefully.

"She's safe." Was all he said.

The leader eyed him menacingly and pointed a fat finger at him.

"I hope for your sake, Martin, that you aren't lying to me."

Martin squared his shoulders holding the fat man's icy gaze but said nothing. After a long moment the leader turned away and began to speak again.

"So how are you going to get the girl to him now?" He asked.

"He already has her." Martin told him.

The leader spun around quickly belying his large stature, a grin spreading over his heavy lips.

"Alright, we should be getting paid very soon then." The leader walked over and slapped Martin on the back.

"Very soon." He said nodding to himself.

Amy woke up again. Her head throbbed with every heart beat.

She slowly propped herself on an elbow and felt the room sway. She lowered herself to the floor again as the room began to spin. Amy opened her eyes but found the room still swaying from side to side. She shut her eyes and breathed in then out slowly to gather her thoughts.

The room was still moving as she opened them. But this time she noticed the erratic movements and heard the noise of something hitting the walls, or what she thought were walls. She sat up slowly and studied the dull lit room.

Then the noise started.

It was loud, painfully loud.

It grew louder in intensity until it seemed to fill the room and engulf her. She covered her ears with her hands and screwed her eyes shut.

She was thrown forward as the noise turned to a scream, the room bouncing around like she was in one of those amusement park rides that made people horribly sick.

A door opened letting daylight flood in. The brightness stung her eyes making them water, she could vaguely see a blurry outline of someone standing in the doorway. Someone huge.

"Good to see you are awake." The figure stated.

Amy cocked her head to one side. The voice sounded wrong, sounded too light. It took a few seconds for her mind to click that the person had been roiding for a very long time.

Amy began to back away into a corner trying to get as far away from the giant as she could.

"I suggest you take the time to get ready. You have a very important meeting." The giant said as it extended a huge arm pointing at another small door.

The figure stepped backwards, the sun almost eclipsed by his outline. The huge arm grabbed the door and half closed it before he paused.

"I wouldn't keep your new employer waiting." He stated, then slammed the door shut.

Amy crawled forward slowly approaching the door. She tried the handle, it was locked. She crawled backwards and jammed herself in the corner as far away from the door as she could.

Chapter 20

"So, where exactly does your relative live?" I asked Dan.

He stayed quiet for a beat as we passed a renovated power station.

"Hamilton." He told me, but offered nothing more.

I looked sideways at him. I had a feeling we were about to walk into something bad.

We drove in silence the rest of the way to the Garden City. My mind drifted around in circles, random thoughts were eventually pushed out by Megan.

I shook my head and sighed. I had to let her go.

I looked across at Dan; he was glancing sideways at me.

"Thinking about her again."

I shook my head and smiled.

"Trying not to."

We reached Hamilton at nine o'clock in the morning.

It was a typical Waikato morning, cold and clear.

Dan drove to the southern side of the city, turned onto the main road out of town that ran past the airport and followed it out. Just before the city line ended and started into the rural area, he hung a left then picked his way slowly up Dixon Road.

Dan pulled over into a space on the side of the road and killed the engine. He looked up the street at a house.

"There it is." He stated pointing up a narrow driveway.

The house was run down and derelict. Straggly vines and plants grew intermixed and spread over the footpath, but that wasn't what got my attention. There was a corrugated fence about ten feet tall, it was painted silver with dark green and brown camouflage, the wrong type for an urban environment. Along the top of it was razor wire, the type they use in military instillations or where something valuable or important is being housed.

I turned in my seat to look at Dan then looked back out the window again.

"Well, this will be interesting." I stated quietly.

As I opened the door I pushed my right hand into my coat and felt the grip of my Beretta. My thumb glided over the safety and hammer to make sure they were in the same positions I had left them when I collected it from its safe.

I stepped onto the sidewalk to survey the area.

It was quiet. The dull roar of traffic from the main road could just be heard over the chill wind that was starting to rise.

I looked up and down the street. There was no real way to approach the fortified house with any degree of stealth. I turned to Dan then started walking.

"Straight up the driveway it is then."

I stepped onto the property. The concrete driveway lead towards the rear and disappeared around the corner of the house. The house was a creamy yellow colour turned dark by years of neglect. The windows were blacked out with either paint or cloth wall hangings. The front door was recessed into the house with a small overhang that provided minimal protection from the weather. I walked up to it and saw a small pen camera peering down at me.

Dan arrived at my side.

"Don't look up but we are being watched." I told him.

He kept his eyes forward then knocked twice on the door, hard.

The sound was dull and flat like the glue holding it together was finally relenting. A creaking noise sounded behind the door then it swung open abruptly.

"What do you want?" The man asked.

I looked at him, his entire face covered in tattoos, a sparse goatee hanging from his chin. He was wearing a vest with the sleeves cut off showing his bulging arms.

His ensemble was topped off with denim jeans and steel capped boots.

Dan stepped up to him and, although shorter, pushed his face into his.

"Martin, where is he?" He asked gnashing his teeth.

I watched the young man visibly stiffen.

The look of superiority returned to his eyes after a second.

The young punk stepped forward trying to back Dan out the door. It didn't work.

"Martin, now." Dan barked.

The young man stopped, unsure of what to do. His eyes darted from Dan's to mine, as if looking for assistance.

He was saved by another voice yelling at him down the hallway.

The young man turned and looked back.

"Just some guys after Martin." The punk called, sounding a lot more timid.

I followed his gaze and saw a man step out of a doorway. He had to turn sideways to pass through it.

I looked at Dan but he was still eyeballing the back of the young mans head. The fat man reached the door and shoved the punk aside. I watched him turn and disappear inside. My gaze fell on the giant blob of a man, his eyes flicking between Dan and I.

His face was free of tattoos but his arms were covered. His clothes only just managed to keep his huge gut contained. I turned and looked back at the street as Dan spoke.

"Martin Wong, where is he?" Dan asked, losing none of the sting in his voice.

The giant looked down at him not bothering to crank his head down.

"No one here by that name." The blob said swinging his gaze at me.

Dan glanced sideways at me then back at the giant.

"He's with me. And don't lie to me. I know he's here, or if he isn't then you know where I can find him." Dan snapped.

The tubby man looked back at Dan.

"You know Daniel, you are in the lions den here." The leader offered with a hint of a grin.

Dan smiled back.

"Try me." He whispered.

The silence intensified until the fat man spoke.

"He's not here."

"Why don't I believe you?" Dan replied.

The fat man shrugged his shoulders then turned to step back inside but Dan grabbed his arm and stopped him. The fat man looked down then directly at him.

Dan stood his ground.

"Get your hand off me." He whispered.

"You tell Martin, if he had anything to do with a girl going missing, I'll put him in the ground." Dan shoved the flabby arm away then turned on his heel to walk back to the street.

I eyed the fat man for a moment then turned and followed.

Out on the street Dan stopped in front of the van and looked down at his hands, they were visibly shaking.

"I think we just made an enemy." He said in a quiet voice.

Chapter 21

"Someone's been sniffing around." Martin told John.

He had secured the girl and she had been shipped off shore. John looked up from his desk, the giant standing behind him, stone still. John nodded, the thumping bass from the club seemed to intensify.

"Well then." John pushed his fingers together forming a triangle as he concentrated on a spot on the plush carpet.

His eyes flicked up and his gaze found Martin.

"Do we know who it is?" John asked.

Martin nodded but didn't reply.

John waited a minute for Martin to answer.

"Well. Who is it?" He asked, frustration rising in his voice.

Martin looked down at the floor then the wall, avoiding eye contact.

John stood up slowly placing his knuckles on the bench and leaned forward slowly.

"I don't appreciate being kept in the dark, Martin. If you say you know who this person is, I want to know about it." John flicked his head without taking his eyes from the biker.

Quicker than Martin thought possible, the giant rounded the desk and had a massive hand clamped around his throat. Martin's eyes bulged from their sockets. He clawed at the giant's arm but the pressure was unrelenting.

"Martin. Are you listening to me?" John asked.

Martin opened his mouth but the words were trapped in his crushed throat. He managed to nod, only once.

"Good. I want you to find this person, I don't care how you do it, but you are to persuade them to stop what they are doing. Is that clear?" John asked casually.

Martin managed to nod again. Bright flashes of light were beginning to explode around the edges of his vision.

The giant held tight.

"Remember Martin, don't fail me."

The giant threw Martin against the far wall where he crashed to the floor gasping for air. The giant stepped past him then pulled the door open indicating for him to leave.

The biker climbed to his feet, his own hand around his throat massaging the bruises that were already beginning to develop. He turned for the door and stumbled towards it.

Martin turned back to say something but saw the giant staring at him, and thought better of it.

As the door slammed closed, Martin made his way to the street. The fledgling headache being compounded by the thumping noise. He climbed onto the Harley and pointed it back towards Hamilton.

"We have a drop to make then we will have run out entirely." The giant told John.

John nodded. He knew if he kept his buyers waiting too long the repercussions could be fatal.

"When is our next delivery?" He asked the giant.

"Three weeks."

John looked up at him.

"The two that are out there at the moment are stretched as far as they can go. We need to get the extra help moving and fast." John told the giant.

The giant nodded and turned to leave.

Then an idea sprang to life.

"Wait." John called after him.

The giant turned back and gazed at John.

"Emery. We could use him to bring in a load to fill the gap until our next shipment arrives." John said, his eyes unfocused in deep thought.

"That sounds dangerous. We don't even know if we can trust him."

John looked up.

"We don't need to trust him; we only need what he has. If he can't get any into the country then we will have to tell our buyers that there won't be any for a while. And he is the cause."

John drummed his fingers on the oak desk as he looked carefully around the room.

"I'll be out there first thing tomorrow morning." John said as he rose slowly from his seat.

The giant shook his head then slammed the door as he strode into the hallway.

John sat down in his seat and looked slowly around the room. He snatched up the receiver to dial Emery's number.

I sat in front of the computer flicking through the police reports for missing persons. Amy Tarrant wasn't listed yet, I guess I was expecting too much.

My cell phone vibrated as it played its annoying tone to get my undivided attention. Snatching it up, the screen showed the number was blocked.

I flicked the screen open.

"Yes." I answered.

"Can you import as well as export?" The voice asked.

The cryptic question caught me off guard and I stumbled for an answer.

"That isn't something I wish to discuss over an open line."

"I'm not sure if you understand me, Emery. You will bring in an amount of my choosing, where and when I specify."

I gnashed my teeth, who did this punk think he was.

"You know I can't do that." I stated.

"I can quadruple your money. All I need is a hundred keys."

I almost laughed but managed to keep it quiet.

"John that's impossible. And you are really taking a risk over an open line like this. I suggest you look elsewhere for what you need." I snapped the phone shut then removed the battery and pulled the SIM card from the slot. I broke it in half then fed it down the drain.

CHAPTER 22

The boat cruised slowly into the bay. The surrounding cliffs offered protection from the ocean swell. The giant looked up at the skipper from the deck and began waving him slowly in to beach the launch on the soft sand. Today the swell had been light and manoeuvring the boat between the jagged rocks at the entrance had been relatively easy. Any significant swell and the boat would have to return to the coast. Which the giant didn't mind but he knew the timetable, the buyers would be here in a matter of weeks. The giant picked up a six metre length of scaffolding wood in one hand then slid one end off the bow of the boat. It tipped over and buried itself in the sand. The giant stepped over the railing and walked down the length of wood with it buckling precariously under his weight. His feet touched the sand and he stopped to breath in a huge lungful of fresh air.

It was peaceful here. The giant loved being on the island, away from the noise of the port and the mainland. He looked up the rising hill in front of him. The tree line started straight off the beach. An area the size of a rugby field had been clear felled to make way for a camp. It was used by various parties as an island getaway or a base from which charters could go fishing from instead of making the four hour trek everyday from the mainland.

Another pair of feet stepped up beside the giant and looked around the sunny cove.

"Nice day for it." The accented voice stated to no one in particular.

The giant just nodded then headed off towards the camp.

Amy awoke to the sound of water gently lapping the side of the boat. She was low enough in the hull to hear it clearly. She focused for a few seconds then realised that all other noise had stopped. The floor remained motionless although the room still swam periodically if she moved her head too fast.

Amy sat up, bright sunlight beamed in through the thinly veiled windows; she squinted and shielded her eyes against the glare.

Slowly she stood up. Her head spun momentarily.

Amy massaged the back of her neck gently trying to relieve the tension that had built up from lying on the rough floor. She finally gazed around the cramped space inside the boat wondering where she was.

Then her hands began to shake.

She looked down, fear flooding back into her.

There was a single knock at the door and it was pushed open. The sunlight that flooded in was quickly blocked by the giant. Amy's eyes adjusted to the brightness as she fixed her gaze upon his face.

What she saw made her skin crawl. He was near bald, skin pulled tight over his face as if it were too small for his skull. His eyes glanced at the door in the corner of the small room.

"I thought I told you to get dressed." He told her.

Amy looked down at her clothes then at the small door then back at the giant in the doorway.

"Where am I?" She asked.

"That doesn't matter, get dressed or I will dress you myself." The giant stated in a monotone.

Amy fixed a hard stare at the man. Defiance blazed in her eyes.

"No." She said quietly.

The giant raised a thick eyebrow.

"Fine, have it your way then." He said as he stepped into the small cabin and slammed the door shut.

John rode in the rear of the limousine to the airport. The sleek black vehicle followed the perimeter road in towards a series of hangers located on the northern edge of the field.

John owned three of them.

The hangers were all painted different colours with names stencilled on the sidewalls that represented the businesses they housed.

They were all fronts though, legitimate businesses, but fronts nonetheless.

The limo pulled to the side of the perimeter road as a four by four slipped past then disappeared around the end of the row of hangers.

The driver stepped out and opened the door for John.

He climbed out then leaned in close to the driver. For anyone watching it would look harmless enough and in fact it was. John told the driver they would return in a few days. He didn't tell the driver any more than that. The driver nodded, walked around the front then climbed into the driver's seat.

John watched the limo leave. It disappeared around the corner of the hangers and left John alone with the noise of jet powered buses flying overhead.

"Are you ready to go Mister Rossi?" John turned to the familiar voice and nodded.

John stepped inside the spacious hanger and cast his gaze at the black Hughes 500 E model. It was sleek; the machine had under gone a face lift. Its nose instead of being rounded was replaced with a wedge bubble.

John stood back and watched the pilot back the helicopter, which was sitting on a small purpose built platform, out of the hanger with a small four wheel ATV.

Another man dressed in overalls walked down a flight of stairs then began to make his way outside. He nodded at John and continued walking towards the helicopter.

John watched the man intently as he pulled a panel open in the engine bay then put his arm inside. After a few seconds the man seemed satisfied that everything was as it should be then closed the panel again.

He shook hands with the pilot and walked back up the stairs closing the door behind him after he stepped into the office on the second floor.

The pilot walked around the helicopter checking various linkages and parts that were vital to the machine staying airborne.

John walked out onto the tarmac. The pilot finished his walk around and unlatched the passenger door for John.

"All ready to go sir." The pilot stated holding the door open.

John climbed inside and began fastening the four point harness. The door clicked quietly closed behind him then the pilot climbed into the left hand seat next to John.

John watched intently as the pilot flicked switches and twisted dials until he was satisfied they read correctly.

The igniters began to crack loudly as the turbine started to whine. Ten seconds later John could barely hear himself think.

He pulled on a headset as the pilot flicked the radio on and pressed the intercom button on the cyclic.

"Should be an uneventful flight out to the island today. We have a slight off shore breeze but it's reasonably smooth." The pilot told John.

The businessman nodded then sat back and waited.

The sleek black 500 screamed past Mount Maunganui sitting at the entrance to the Tauranga harbour.

John looked down at the ocean, he was amazed that after all these years it could still lure him back. He loved the ocean, loved everything about it. It held mystery and unknowns. It could be loving and cruel, life giving and life taking. But for John it had always been a source of relaxation. Somewhere he could be alone and at ease with his thoughts.

John scanned the cluster of instruments in front of him. He understood most of them and what they represented. The altimeter told him they were currently at two thousand feet above sea level.

It didn't look that far.

John looked off to the east. He could see the coast line stretch away before him. The surf tumbled onto the fine sand releasing a salty mist to the breeze creating a haze that all but obscured the far reaches of the coast from sight.

"Should take us about twenty minutes to reach the island." The pilot stated through the intercom.

John nodded and glanced at the gauges again.

The helicopter touched down in a cleared area of forest, the pilot skilfully manoeuvred the machine down into the rough clearing between the canopy of the trees.

The descent was about thirty metres before the skids came to rest on the prepared pad cut into the undergrowth. The pilot cut the fuel to the engine and waited for the blades to stop spinning before he climbed out.

John pushed open the passenger door and dropped down onto the lumpy ground. The soil was dry but dark, mixed with volcanic rock. John looked through the trees and could see nothing but forest.

Dark lumps of jagged rock broke the surface of the ground at abrupt angles.

John's watch said nine AM. He planned on being here all day and wanted to get started. It was then he heard a twig snap, he looked up abruptly.

"Good morning." The giant stated in his light voice.

"I trust the ride out was smooth?" He asked.

John nodded then turned to look at the pilot.

"Are we ready?" He asked, which the pilot knew was code for him to hurry up.

The pilot nodded and finished tying down the rotor blades then retrieved a pack from the rear seat.

"Ok, let's go." John said to the giant.

Chapter 23

I parked the rental car in a vacant spot on Ohaupo road and climbed out into the cold clear day.

It was early, around six thirty to be exact. I wanted to catch Martin off guard. He knew something, I wanted to find out what it was.

I stepped onto the sidewalk then began heading down the hill towards the last street on the left. I hadn't told Dan what I was doing; I wanted to leave him out of it.

I carefully scanned the street, it was quiet and no one was out. Winter leaves lay scattered dead on the foot path. I reached the road, my fingers touched the small of my back, the Beretta still in the same place exactly as I had positioned it.

I turned up the street and began walking, a jogger ran past on the opposite side of the road. Female, she looked about twenty five although it is hard to tell from a distance.

I glanced in her direction as she looked across the street at me, she carried on thinking nothing of it.

I reached the entrance to the gang headquarters and turned up the broken concrete driveway. A curtain moved in one of the windows to my left. I slowed a fraction then carried on towards the door.

As I reached the steps to the front door it swung open, a young man stood in the doorway. He was wearing a hoodie over top of a peaked hat. A black bandana covered his nose and mouth, dark glasses covered his eyes.

"What you want?" The gruff voice asked.

I looked at him then past him down the hallway. The fat man we had talked to previously stood at the opposite end of the hallway with his arms folded across his chest. There was a smirk on his face.

I looked back at the young punk in front of me.

"Martin, now." I said quietly.

If the icy edge in my voice had any effect he didn't show it. Instead he stepped forward, closing the distance between us.

I could smell him, the stench of days on end without bathing.

"He's not here, now leave." The punk told me.

I could hear anger in his voice beginning to boil.

I shook my head and said nothing.

"Leave now!" The punk yelled at me.

I looked past him at the fat man in the hallway; the smirk was gone, replaced with a hard look. My eyes flicked back to the young punk on front of me.

"LEAVE NOW!" He screamed.

I shook my head and stood my ground. The young guy stepped closer, his nose inches from mine. I could hear him grinding his teeth.

"If you don't leave now, you will be a dead man."

I levelled my eyes at him.

He was too close so I stepped backwards.

At the same time my hands came up grabbing the scruff of his shirt. My foot fell to the lower step, I twisted hard pulling the punk off balance as he followed me down the step. As he fell past me, I shoved him hard onto the cracked concrete where he skidded to a halt. I turned back to the doorway in time to see the fat man coming towards me. He wasn't interested in talking anymore.

Neither was I.

I stepped onto the landing then launched at the doorway.

I was through being polite, I wanted answers.

The fat man hesitated for a fraction of a second. I brought my fist up and caught the leader square in the centre of his oversized belly. He folded forward, a great whoosh of air escaped his mouth. I bent down a fraction next to him.

"Martin, where is he?" I whispered.

The leader tried to speak but all that came out were croaks and splutters.

I pulled my fist from his stomach and turned in time to see the young punk climbing to his feet. I could see a look of hate in his body. He took a step forward then froze.

"Don't." I told him.

The Beretta aiming at his face.

I looked down at the fat man on his hands and knees.

"All I want is to talk to Martin, nothing difficult about that." I told them.

The young punk looked briefly at the fat man then back at me.

"Wait." The fat man wheezed.

He pulled himself up by the door frame and regained his composure.

He turned in the hallway without taking his eyes off me and yelled.

"Martin. Get out here now."

I kept the Beretta firmly pointed at the young punk. I could hear soft foot falls in the hallway then stop. Slowly I lowered the pistol.

"All I want is a word with Martin then I will leave." I told them.

"What do you want?" Martin asked from the hallway.

"Information." I told him. "About the girl you are trying to find."

"Turns out she's dead. I found her in the hospital morgue." Martin told me matter-of-factly.

I turned towards him not believing a word.

I said nothing for a moment.

"That's not what I heard." I stated.

A smile spread across Martin's thin lips.

"What did you hear then?" He asked.

I looked at him and decided to take a gamble. If he knew something he would show it.

"She's been kidnapped. Someone broke into her house, killed her flatmate then snatched her." I removed the small piece of rag from my pocket, the piece we found at Amy's house, and showed it to him.

Martin, to his credit, stayed still, completely still. It was the fat man beside him that gave him away. His eyes flickered then glanced at Martin.

"I'm willing to bet that there will be something on this rag that you drugged the girl with. I'm also willing to bet that if I looked through the house I would find the knife you used to slit the other girls throat with." I said pointing at the house.

"That would be an unwise move on your part, Emery." Martin said quietly.

I held his gaze until he broke away.

"You've got it all wrong Emery. She's not here, like I told you she's in the morgue." He stated finally.

He stepped past the leader and eyed me.

"Now I suggest you leave before we call the police and have them arrest you for trespassing."

The leader was standing in the doorway grinning again thinking he had regained the upper hand. I nodded then turned and walked towards the street holstering my Beretta before I stepped onto the sidewalk.

Chapter 24

Melissa stepped into the morgue, the harsh lights reflecting brightly off the stainless steel panels and stark white floor tiles. The strong smell of ammonia hung in the air disguising the underlying odour of death.

And it was cold.

The medical examiner crossed the room to a wall with steel doors. He went through a list looking at the numbers. He found the one he was looking for then pulled the door open without hesitation.

The M.E. looked at Melissa then grabbed the white sheet and pulled it back.

The body on the tray was naked. Her blonde hair lay trapped under her shoulders. Melissa turned to the M.E.

"How did she die?" She asked.

He flipped a few pages and found a record.

"Massive overdose of this new synthetic drug thats just started circulating. I've heard from colleagues overseas that its ten times the strength of what's normally available. I guess she was never told about it." He stated indicating to the damaged veins under her skin after he picked up her arm.

Melissa pulled a small camera from her pocket.

"You mind?" She asked.

The M.E. gently placed the arm back on the steel tray and indicated for her to do whatever she needed.

Melissa paid particular attention to her arms and face. She shot close ups of her hair and face structure.

"She also has a small tattoo on the inside of her left ankle." The M.E. stated as he pulled the cloth lower.

Melissa moved around the side of the steel table then took a close up of the ink. It was a small butterfly resting on a twig. Its red wings a stark contrast against the milky white skin.

"Is that the only identifying mark?" Melissa asked.

The M.E. nodded.

Melissa looked down at the body and wondered what she must have endured before she died. She shook her head to rid the images that began to invade her mind and turned to leave.

"Thanks." She said over her shoulder.

I pulled into the car parking building of the hospital and paid the hideously expensive charge. Not surprisingly the car park was mostly empty. I locked the rental and walked towards the entrance. The hospital was undergoing extensive renovations to make it look and feel more friendly and welcoming. The sliding glass doors rolled open to reveal a brand new reception area.

I looked across the foyer at a receptionist busily typing something into a computer. I read the signs above the various hallways and lifts that transited the hospital campus.

People were walking in pairs and singles, in and out of various doors and entrance ways. I studied a few and saw a woman looking sideways at me. Her honey blonde hair was tied back in a ponytail, her piercing blue eyes stayed locked on mine.

The woman was dressed in a pants suit with a crisp white shirt and a dark navy jacket.

As she walked past me her jacket flapped open, I caught a flash of brass. Her gaze broke away then she stepped out into the parking building disappearing from sight.

I stored the mental image away, somehow I felt that it wouldn't be the last time we would cross paths.

I walked slowly towards an entrance and continued on until I found another corridor with a sign that gave me several different directions to take for different departments. It didn't list the morgue.

It wasn't something the hospital wanted the general public to have immediate access to.

I tracked back down the long hallway with a red line running down its centre as a person came rushing towards me. She was holding a clip board and furiously turning pages. She had an ID clipped to her belt, her eyes focused on the pages in front of her.

"Excuse me Ma'am. I'm looking for the morgue." I stated as she neared me.

She stopped looking up abruptly.

"What?" She asked.

"The morgue, I'm here to identify a body." I replied as I flashed my fake police badge.

"Reception should be able to help you." She said pointing the way she was headed. Her name was Kathy, her almost black hair and eyes a startling contrast against her pale skin. She wore an engagement ring on her left hand, her nails painted black.

"They told me to talk to you." I lied.

Kathy looked up again then past me at the receptionist then back at me.

"It's off limits to the public." She stated, this time hugging the clipboard to her chest.

"Like I said, I'm only here to identify a body. Just doing my job."

I could see her debating with herself.

Quickly she turned around to check behind her then stepped past me without saying a word. I turned to watch her go, it was then I realised she was taking me there.

She led me out the main entrance to a ring road, turned right and followed the footpath past the gardens and construction zones. I caught up to her and fell in step along side her.

"You're here to identify a body." She stated more than asked.

I nodded but didn't reply.

"When exactly did the body arrive at the morgue?" She asked.

I kept pace beside her and thought of a quick answer.

"I'm not sure. I was only told this morning to get down here." I told her.

She nodded staying quiet for a beat.

"Who was it supposed to be?" Kathy asked.

"Just a missing person reported a few weeks ago." I replied.

Kathy stopped abruptly to turn then look at me.

"Who did you say you worked for again?" She asked.

"Police." I lied again.

She nodded then turned and carried on towards the morgue.

We stepped inside the mortuary, there was a lot of frosted glass and dark hardwood. I guessed it was an effort to make the place feel warm and inviting, but the temperature dropped as we crossed the threshold. Kathy walked to the reception desk and up to a guy dressed in a white lab coat. I followed behind casually glancing around the area.

"This officer is here to ID a body." Kathy told the tall man in the lab coat. The man looked at me then asked.

"Male or female?"

"Female."

"Are there any distinguishing marks on her body?"

"I'm not sure."

The man in the lab coat looked at me then added.

"It would help if you knew who you were supposed to be looking for."

I thought quickly.

"She has blonde hair, shoulder length, dark eyes. Her age is twenty two, she is around five foot five."

Kathy gazed at me as I answered, I had the unsettling feeling she knew I was winging it. The man in the lab coat looked down at the register and flicked to the last page.

"We have already had an officer come in here. She told me exactly the same characteristics."

Out of the corner of my eye I could see Kathy's shoulders slump.

I said nothing.

"This way." The man in the lab coat said.

He spun on his heel and pushed through a heavy steel door that made a sucking sound as it opened.

The temperature dropped further then the stench hit me. The overpowering smell of industrial strength bleach barely masking the sickening smell of death. The man in the lab coat walked to a steel door then yanked it open. He knew why I was here and who I was here to see. He lifted the sheet back to reveal the body.

The first thing I noticed were the needle tracks on her arms. Her skin looked pale and gaunt, not the skin of someone who was otherwise healthy.

"She also has a tattoo on her left ankle." The man said as he removed the sheet to show me.

I glanced sideways to see Kathy gazing at the body with sadness in her eyes.

I nodded, I'd seen enough.

I thanked Kathy and the man in the lab coat then headed for the door.

Chapter 25

R ossi had been tramping for what seemed like hours. He kept quiet though, in reality they had only been moving for forty five minutes.

The giant stopped and removed a well worn map from one of his pockets. He knew his way around the island so didn't really need the map. He took a bottle of water and a pill bottle from a small pouch then palmed four pills into his mouth and washed them down with a mouthful of water.

They walked for another hour, the watery sun failed to penetrate the tall canopy keeping the temperature cool.

They reached a small wooden hut near the centre of the island. It looked like it had been built a significant number of years prior then been abandoned. The boards were weather beaten a dirty grey colour. The roof was intact, it had been patched up where it was needed but for the most part it was as they had found it.

Until they stepped inside.

The walls were lined with thick new plywood, it had made the small structure extremely solid. Along one side was a small desk with a chair and a lamp on the table, next to it was a medium size steel cabinet.

In the very centre of the floor was a wooden trap door with a large steel lock holding it closed.

The giant removed a key from his pocket then jammed the key into the lock and twisted. It let go with a resounding click. He pulled the lock free, handed it to the pilot then lifted the door out of its indentation.

The smell of damp earth mixed with the sharp stench of isopropyl alcohol wafted up out of the brightly lit stairwell. The giant indicated for Rossi to lead.

John had descended the stairs many times, every time he did he could feel a primal fear begin to creep through him that he knew was irrational, but it was there nonetheless.

It would be just the two of them now. Only the giant and he had access to the tunnel. The pilot shut the door behind them, Rossi heard the lock click into place then felt his fear creep a notch higher, as it always did.

The stairs descended close to a hundred metres. It was a long walk, John could feel the temperature rise.

They stopped at another landing with a door in front of them, the giant slipped past John then slid another key into a lock, he shoved the heavy door aside.

The cavern was huge, the size of half a football field wide and long. The ceiling was close to a fifty feet high.

The whole area had been blasted and carved out of solid volcanic rock.

John stepped out into the brightly lit area. Someone rushed past carrying a large steel tray with strips of different coloured paper laid out in a sequence, an Ingram machine pistol slung over his shoulder.

John knew it was for a PH test.

Litmus paper designed to test for acid or alkali levels. If the paper turned red or a shade of red then it meant acid was present, the same was true for alkali, only the paper turned blue.

The giant stepped through the door way then slammed it shut as if it weighed nothing at all.

The large area was full of chaos. People were scurrying back and forth carrying various trays and weapons.

To one side were long runs of tables supporting various pieces of equipment used in the process of cutting the powder.

The stench of alcohol and acid mixed with the sharp smell of the powder being cooked produced a suffocating gas which left the people feeling sick at the end of the day. John had discovered this during the first week of production, he had ordered large extraction fans be put in the roof to remove the toxic fumes.

The giant and a team had bored three large holes through the rock to facilitate the instillation of an extraction system. The system removed most of the toxic fumes but Rossi could still feel a headache coming on.

Rossi eyed the new recruit at one table carefully but very slowly separating contents on the table in front of her. Her eyes were red rimmed, her hair ragged and unkempt. She looked out of place in the cavern. She was in a summer dress, like someone who should be at the beach but somehow ended up in a nightmare. An armed guard stood next to her, watching her every move carefully. He had a pistol in one hand, his arms folded across his chest, his face devoid of emotion.

"Did she give you any trouble?" Rossi asked.

The giant grinned.

"Nothing I couldn't handle." He replied quietly.

Rossi nodded then walked around the end of the long row of tables and carefully inspected each member of the processing team as he went.

The product needed to be good, very good.

Rossi knew if the product wasn't the utmost top quality his operation would be terminated, along with him and everyone in the cavern.

This he drilled into his employees. If they didn't perform to expectations their life would become very difficult.

And this was the conversation he was about to have with their new chemist, Amy Tarrant.

Chapter 26

Martin watched Emery as he walked down the cracked driveway towards the road. He balled his fists and ground his teeth together. Emery knew something but couldn't prove anything. He sure as hell wouldn't find her unless he got really lucky.

Martin shook his head and turned to walk back inside but was blocked by the fat leader. The grin was gone which had been replaced with a troubled look.

"You were told not to bring anything here." The fat man stated.

Martin said nothing, he knew his place but was beginning to think the fat man didn't.

"Don't threaten me. If you hadn't tried to act like such a tough guy I could have thrown him off the trail. But now he knows something is up. He is going to check the story about the girl in the morgue. You're just lucky that I managed to get the corpse from somewhere else. Someone who died as a result of your employers drugs." Martin said jabbing him in the chest with his finger.

The fat man looked down at Martin's hand then gazed back into his eyes, his stare cold and hard.

"Touch me again and I will kill you, Martin." The fat man whispered.

Martin stood his ground for a moment then realised that he had overstepped the mark. He dropped his gaze to the ground then looked back up slowly.

"I'll take care of Emery." He said.

The leader said nothing, only held his gaze. After a long uncomfortable pause the leader spoke.

"And what about your so called relation?"

Martin paused then nodded.

"Him too." He added.

The fat man turned and walked back into the run down house. He didn't bother closing the door behind him, he knew Martin would be inside soon.

Martin turned on the stone steps to look at the pathetic little punk staring at him.

"Take that shit off your face, you look like an idiot." Martin yelled.

He turned and stormed inside.

Martin sat down in the kitchen to think about his next move.

He could try to remove the problem but he knew that would be a fatal idea. He had researched Emery and what little he had found about him told Martin that it didn't bode well for anyone who messed with him.

Still he had to do something.

Martin decided he would put a bounty on Emery's head and take care of Dan himself.

He lifted his phone from the table then flicked the screen open. The keys beeped unobtrusively as he pressed the phone number in slowly and deliberately.

It was answered on the fourth ring.

"Yes?" The voice asked.

"I have a job." Martin replied.

Martin listened; he could hear the man eating, a television playing quietly in the background.

"Ok. I'll be at the corner of Grey and Clyde in twenty minutes." The man severed the connection.

Martin clicked his shut.

He stood quickly and without saying anything, disappearing through the back door.

Martin blasted through a red light, cutting off a car which elicited angry gestures and extended blasts from people's horns.

He ignored them.

If he really wanted to he could own this town but he knew that would bring no end of grief, paranoia and violence.

And he knew violence was best left in the hands of those who were good at it.

Martin stopped at the traffic lights on Grey Street, the Harley thumped away while he scanned the sidewalks. It didn't take him long to spot his contact.

Although Martin knew he would never see this guy coming if the tables were turned, he was thankful that he was on his side.

Martin crossed to the sidewalk slowly and pulled the Harley to the side of the street causing traffic to swerve around him. He took his helmet off then kicked the bike over onto the side stand.

Martin looked up at his contact. He wasn't overly big or tall. The man had hair shaved close to his head, his glasses were the type that darkened in the sunlight. He was dressed in jeans and a buttoned shirt covered by a thin leather jacket. To anyone on the street he looked like any other person going about his business.

Martin knew different though.

The man looked down at Martin.

"Can we make this quick." The man stated.

Martin nodded.

"The guy's name is Emery Blackstone." Martin told the man.

He just nodded then asked.

"Timeframe?"

"As soon as possible. He is giving us some trouble."

The man nodded again.

"Ok, it's the standard fee."

Martin pulled his helmet on then pushed the starter button. He waited for a gap in the traffic then pulled out into the flow.

He looked in his rear-view mirror, the man stepped into the flow of traffic to cross the street towards town.

Martin knew from experience that Emery was about to have a very difficult time.

Chapter 27

Amy stood at a metal bench. She ached all over. Large splotchy bruises were beginning to form on her arms and legs. The giant had been overly rough with her, forcibly putting the dress on her. She had fought hard all the way refusing to do what she was told.

But it was no use.

So she tore the dress off her shoulders and screamed at the top of her lungs. The giant jammed his hands over his ears waiting for her to stop. Amy had run out of breath, the scream eventually fading to nothing.

The giant took one step towards her then slapped her hard across the face knocking her to the floor. She tried to open her eyes but couldn't see anything. They were blurred.

"Get dressed." The giant yelled at her.

Amy lay naked on the floor spitting blood.

It wasn't until much later that she was introduced to the lab.

Now Amy stood at a metal bench, a tray in front of her loaded with off white rocks. She knew what it was and wanted nothing to do with it. Her left eye was swollen shut and her jaw hurt like nothing she had ever felt before.

Amy looked up slowly; a man dressed in a suit was walking purposefully towards her.

"Amy. I'm John Rossi." The man stated formally as he extended his hand.

Amy looked out of the corner of her open eye saying nothing in return.

John pulled a metal chair from under the table and offered it to her then sat in another facing her.

Amy ignored it.

"Why am I here?" She asked suddenly.

"Because you have a talent and we have an opportunity for you to use that talent." He indicated to the rock walls.

Amy looked down at the uncut drugs in front of her.

"I refuse to touch this." She whispered to Rossi.

"I see."

John turned in his seat and looked at one of the armed guards then nodded.

Quickly the man rushed towards Amy and jammed a pistol to the side of her head. He gripped her shoulder then spun her to face a dark door seated flush in the rock face. The guard shoved her along the rough surface saying nothing.

Amy's head was bent over to the left; she could feel the muscles in her neck begin to cramp as the pressure became too much.

The man reached the door and opened it. He pushed her inside then flicked a light switch. A single bulb over head began to burn brightly. Amy saw the chair sitting in the middle of the room and began to squirm.

The guard gripped her shoulder tighter and shoved her into the chair, the pistol still against her temple.

"Hands behind the chair, now." The guard told her.

Amy didn't move.

"Hands, NOW!" the guard yelled at her.

Amy screwed her eyes shut and whimpered at the harshness in his voice but she didn't move.

"Ok, have it your way." The guard said then turned and walked out of the room slamming the door shut.

Amy opened her eyes slowly to gaze around the room. It was claustrophobic, wet and dank. When she saw water seeping from the walls she instantly began to shiver, whether it was from the building fear or the cold, she wasnt sure. She wondered how long she would have to wait, her thoughts began racing.

She didn't have to wait long.

The door opened and the giant man who had bruised her filled the doorway. He stepped in then to one side as the man called John Rossi followed. He slammed the door shut and stood looking at Amy.

John nodded to the giant.

Amy watched as the giant moved around behind her grabbing a wrist in a vice like grip. She wriggled on the seat and stood up. The giant twisted her arm then tucked it under his jamming her between his massive forearm and even larger torso.

Her hand was stretched out in front of him while her head was jammed hard against his back. Amy screamed and struggled but his grip only tightened. John stepped around behind the giant then bent down to look Amy in the eyes.

"You will work for us Ms Tarrant." John stated.

Amy shook her head.

"No, I won't do it." She screamed.

John looked at her as a wicked grin spread across his face.

"Oh I think you will, Amy."

Rossi stood up slowly then walked around the giant. Amy struggled but it was useless. She couldn't move.

"I think you will Amy. You don't really have any other option."

John nodded at the giant and Amy felt one hand release its grip. She struggled but it was to no avail.

The giant clamped down on her right index finger. Amy could feel the pressure build in her finger tip; it felt like it was ready to pop.

"I have found this to be a very effective form of persuasion."

Amy began to panic.

Something grazed the tip of her finger as she struggled, she froze in terror.

"This is Inconel lock wire. It's extremely strong and tough. When cut its edges are very sharp, it has a tendency to embed itself under the skin if one isn't paying attention. The coating attacks the cells in the skin causing them to turn sore." Rossi explained as he placed the sharp edge against her fingertip.

The wire slipped under Amy's finger nail with very little effort. Rossi pushed it in until the tip disappeared under the cuticle.

Amy sucked in a large breath then screamed. The noise echoed off the stone walls reverberating and accentuating the high pitch noise.

Rossi screwed his eyes shut then quickly withdrew the wire. Amy's eyes jammed open but before she had a chance to scream again John clamped a hand over her mouth.

"Now, Ms Tarrant, you will work for us, or, we can continue down this path." John whispered to her.

Her eyes darted around the room, sweat running from her hair line. She screwed her eyes shut and concentrated on the pain radiating up her arm.

She nodded.

"Remember that pain Amy, next time it will be a lot worse." John slowly took his hand away as the giant let go, Amy collapsed to the floor.

The giant stepped through the door followed by Rossi. He stopped in the doorway.

"You have ten minutes, then you will get to work."

He stepped into the cavern leaving the door open for her.

Amy lay still on the floor, her hand throbbing. A tiny droplet of blood beaded on the end of her finger dropping to the stone floor.

Amy gazed at her finger through watering eyes then pulled her arms and legs up and curled into a ball as her sobs echoed through the rock cavern.

CHAPTER 28

Melissa sat at her desk in the Manukau police station. She was leaning forward over the key board typing furiously trying to remember the details. She was logged onto a secure server relaying information back to the DEA. She knew the body in the morgue wasn't the missing girl Amy, her parents had told her vehemently their daughter was not and would never use drugs. They also knew nothing about a tattoo on her ankle.

'Amy simply wouldn't do that.' Her mother had told Melissa, and she believed her.

Melissa hit enter then waited for a reply.

It took five minutes for it to come through. Melissa sighed in frustration; it was the same as always. Keep looking, we are doing everything we can here to pin point where the drugs are coming from but we are running into political pressure.

Melissa typed a short reply then pressed enter, she shut the computer down.

It was late and she was tired.

The station house was bathed in the dull glow of screen savers that had been left on for the night. Melissa collected her coat from the back of her chair then headed for the elevator that would take her to the underground car park.

She hit the speed bump at the car park enterence then turned onto Wiri Station Road. The drive was short, traffic was light and the green lights played in her favour.

Melissa parked on the street, climbed out then locked her car.

Her rented flat was sparsely furnished with only what she needed.

Melissa had been told her stay would be no longer than two months.

That was three months ago.

Her frustration was beginning to get the better of her and it was showing more and more every day.

She dumped her bag on the small table then dropped herself onto the lumpy couch in the darkness. Melissa sat still, her mind scrolled over the days events.

Only two things stood out to her.

One, the girl in the morgue at Hamilton hospital was not Amy Tarrant, and two, the stranger she crossed paths with in the reception area.

Melissa pulled herself up then walked to a small desk and pressed the power button on a small laptop. It took a minute for it to warm up then bring up its screen.

Melissa decided she would go searching.

The first name she typed in the search engine was Nick Baker.

She hit enter.

The screen redrew with a list of pages she could visit for various people whose names were Nick Baker. She read through some of the captions and found Nick Baker the cop.

It was a face book page.

Melissa clicked on it, the screen redrew to the entry page.

She navigated her way through to find Nick's home page.

The photo showed him standing in front of a white wall; he was dressed in his uniform with dark glasses.

Melissa clicked on the photo to enlarge it to make absolutely sure it was him.

Next she browsed the information pages. It told her he had twenty friends listed. Melissa brought up the list but couldn't see anyone that took her interest; she closed the page then typed Amy Tarrant into the search engine.

The search engine spat out an article about Amy.

She looked at the screen and frowned.

They hadn't finished the investigation yet and she knew Amy wasn't dead.

The body in the morgue was not her.

"So who told everyone you were dead?" She asked herself.

Melissa clicked the article to read it from start to finish. The article stated that she was found dead in her flat after a drug overdose. Her flatmate had arrived home to find her dead on the bedroom floor.

This didn't make sense.

When she and Baker searched the flat there was only one body, that body was not Amy Tarrant. The body was identified as

Karen James. She closed the page and brought up the New Zealand Herald website. She found the contact details then dialled the phone number.

She asked to speak to the reporter who wrote the article about Amy.

"Yes." Came the gruff greeting after she was transferred.

"I'm Melissa Cross with the Manukau police. I'd like to ask you a few questions regarding the article you ran on Amy Tarrant."

There was a pause then the reporter answered.

"Ok, but make it quick. I have a dead line tomorrow morning and I'm well behind." The voice stated.

Melissa balled her fist around the phone cord and mentally told herself to calm down.

"When did you write the article?" She asked.

"The date is at the top." The voice replied.

"That isn't the question I asked. When did you write the article?" She asked again, her voice clipped.

A sigh echoed out of the receiver telling her that he really didn't have time to be answering stupid questions that the police were too incompetent to answer themselves.

"It would have been the day before." The voice told her curtly.

"And who gave you the information?" She asked.

There was a sharp intake of air and the voice scoffed.

"If you think I am going to give up my sources, lady, you are sadly mistaken."

"If that's how you really feel, I'm sorry to hear that. But I must insist, if you don't assist the police with a murder investigation you will be arrested for obstruction, and I'm sure if I tried really hard, I could find something else to add to the list." Melissa replied sweetly.

"You can't do that…" Melissa cut him off.

"All you need to do is tell me who you got your information from."

The voice stayed quiet for several seconds.

"Baker. A cop called Baker." The voice told her.

The line went dead.

Melissa looked at the receiver then slowly lowered it to the cradle.

"What the hell?" She breathed.

Now she had some questions that needed answering.

Chapter 29

Dan pulled into the driveway as I opened the door to step outside. It was dark.

He shut the engine off then opened the door. He stepped out of the van then slowly walked towards me.

"What's wrong?" I asked.

"I had a visit last night. Someone came to me looking for you. They know we know each other."

"Did this person have a name?" I asked.

Dan shook his head.

"But I have seen him before. Years ago." Dan sighed.

I looked at him.

"Well don't keep me in suspense."

"He's an assassin. And he's coming after you." He said with some finality.

I looked at him then began to laugh.

"Is that it? For a moment I thought you were going to tell me Roxie had died." I said as I turned to walk back inside.

I set the kettle going then pulled two cups from the cupboard, placing them on the bench. I dropped a tea bag into one and a spoonful of coffee into the other.

I turned to Dan.

"What did this guy look like?" I asked.

"Nothing spectacular. Close cropped hair. Wore wire rimmed glasses. Not overly huge but he looked kind of intense." He stated from the dining room table.

A smile grew over my face.

"Sounds like my kind of guy." I mumbled as I poured boiling water into the cups.

I placed the cup in front of Dan then sat down.

"It doesn't make sense. Why would he come to see me if he knew I would give you a warning?"

"Because he isn't going to kill me." I told him.

Dan looked at me.

"How do you know that?" He asked arching an eyebrow.

I said nothing.

Dan picked up his cup then took a sip.

My mind scrolled back to the years the assassin and I spent in the trenches. It had been hell. We saw people die all around us, friends and enemies.

Images of blood stained dirt flooded my mind, it took me several seconds to realise that Dan was saying something.

"Sorry what did you say?" I asked as I shook my head.

"What exactly are you going to do? I mean you can't start another fire fight here."

I looked at him.

"First off, I'm not going to do anything. The assassin will come to me and second I didn't start any fire fight. Jacob did that remember, it almost got me killed."

Dan looked down at his coffee staying quiet for a spell.

"Just watch your back Emery. This guy seems, well, seems cold. Like he won't stop." I nodded.

Dan was correct to think that, the assassin wouldn't stop. But I knew, as sure as the sun would come up tomorrow that he wouldn't kill me.

I nodded and told him I would be careful. Dan drained his cup and headed for the door. He stopped at the door as if he was going to say something then didn't, he just left.

The next morning, I rose late.

I touched the power button on the computer.

I wanted to read the morning papers before I drove to Tauranga to deliver the news to John. I was going to tell him that I could deliver on the drugs but it would take four weeks to arrive.

The newspapers were littered with the usual.

Gang violence, murders, drugs.

To find anything worth reading, it was usually buried a few pages in.

The drive to Tauranga was slow. I was taking the gorge road through Paeroa and Waihi.

The traffic, slow and heavy causing frustration.

I idled past two men standing on the side of the road arguing heatedly, oblivious to the traffic rolling past them.

I crawled across the bridge into Paeroa township then straight through the intersection pulling up to the petrol pumps of a service station.

The wind was blowing and cold.

A southerly had picked up and was making itself felt.

As I stepped into the breeze another car pulled up tight behind me. I eyed the driver then paid him no attention.

There were no other cars on the forecourt.

As the shop doors slid open, I was hit by a blast of warm air.

I looked around and saw two cameras watching me as I walked towards the counter.

I paid the attendant for the gas and brought an orange juice before heading back to my car.

The filler went in, I stood watching the pump register, dollars clicking twice as fast as litres.

The car behind me was still pulled up tight to the rear bumper.

I looked at the guy again to see he was talking on a cell phone.

He looked at me then looked across the road at something.

I followed his gaze but only saw vehicles.

The pump clicked off then I pulled the filler out and closed the gas cap. I pushed the filler into the pump housing then slowly I climbed in the driver's door and pulled it closed.

It was then that I realised something was very, very wrong.

CHAPTER 30

Melissa stepped through the door into the warmth of the squad room. She walked to her desk and draped her coat over the back of her seat. She casually glanced around to see Nick sitting at his desk looking flustered. She wanted to wait until the right time to spring her questions on him.

The Captain walked out of his office, beelined towards Nick and handed him a sheaf of paper then looked across the room at Melissa.

Nick's shoulders slumped.

He stood and walked towards her after Tony had returned to his office. He reached her desk then stopped and sighed dramatically.

"There's been an explosion at a petrol station." He told her.

Melissa kept quiet waiting for more information. Nick looked at her stupidly. Melissa grew impatient.

"I assume you are telling me this for a reason?" She asked.

Nick blinked.

"Yes, Tony told us to go and deal with it." Nick stated as he turned away.

Melissa rolled her eyes then stood to gather her coat.

The squad car bumped over the curb. The flames had kept most people well back, the fire crews had pushed them back even further.

Roads had been closed disrupting traffic. Melissa climbed out of the car and was instantly assaulted by five different news crews. She waved them away but they were insistent on getting their sound bites. Melissa stepped under the tape and was greeted by a fireman walking towards her. She flashed her badge as did Nick.

"Officers." The man said in greeting.

"What happened here?" Nick asked.

"We will know more once the area is void of hot spots. But it looks like static discharge ignited vapours as a car was refuelling."

Melissa looked down the street. She could see smoke coiling into the sky from the damaged awning above the destroyed vehicles.

Two fire appliances had arrived and swiftly estinguished the flames before the underground tanks had caught limiting the potentially massive damage. Clumps of foam floated across the street from giant hoses that had drowned the burnt out vehicles.

"How many people were involved?" Melissa asked as she pulled out a small note book.

"There were two cars on the forecourt; both were occupied at the time of the explosion which engulfed both cars. No one has come forward so we are assuming the worst. We should know more soon." The fireman stated as he turned to look back at the blackened wrecks.

It took fifteen minutes to make sure there were no hot spots that could reignite. During that time Melissa, followed by Nick, walked closer to the scene. She wanted to be there as soon as the scene was cleared.

It didn't take long for her to ascertain there was only one fatality. The person in the front vehicle was slumped over the steering wheel with the other car close to the rear bumper. Melissa could tell it wouldn't have taken much for the second car to catch fire. She kept her distance; she wanted to take in the whole area.

The blackened, charred shells of the cars were sagged on warped springs.

Nothing was left.

The fire had been intensely hot scorching the concrete immediately around the pumps and burning the grass on the sidewalk.

Melissa turned slowly on the spot to take in the immediate area. An ambulance was parked behind the engines.

She could see a young man in the rear with an oxygen mask over his nose and mouth while a paramedic covered his arm with a bandage. Melissa walked slowly towards the ambulance and flashed her badge as she neared.

"That looks nasty." She stated, looking down at his arm.

He winced as the paramedic finished the bandage off with a piece of tape to hold it in place.

"Hurts like hell." He said around the oxygen mask.

"What happened?" She asked with genuine concern in her voice.

The young guy looked up at her then removed the mask so he could speak clearly and gazed over at the charred wreck.

"A guy came in to get some fuel. Walked inside to pay for it, the pumps are on prepay. We've had so many thefts over the last year we didn't really have a choice. He buys an orange juice and forty dollars of fuel then goes outside, puts the nozzle into the tank and stands there waiting for it to finish. It finishes because I can see it on the till as the pump stops. He hangs it back up, climbs into the car then, boom. The car gets blown all to hell."

Melissa wrote in her note book then looked across the road at the scene.

"What about the other person in the car behind it. Must have been someone in there?" She asked. The guy nodded.

"Yeah there was, but when I went outside to see if I could put the fire out he had disappeared."

Melissa wrote this down; she could feel the beginnings of something coming together.

"What did he look like?" She asked.

The young guy shook his head and was quiet for a moment.

"I don't really remember, he just sat there. I guess he was waiting for the guy to shift but the rest of the forecourt was empty. There were half a dozen other pumps available." The young guy stated.

"I only glanced outside, didn't really take any notice, sorry." He carried on.

Melissa must have looked disappointed because the young guy said something else.

"Maybe the video footage would be of better help."

Melissa looked up at him.

"Does it cover the forecourt?" She asked.

"And inside. You could probably get a better look at the guy who died. The cameras over the till are pointed straight at the customers face."

Melissa smiled; she felt a glimmer of hope.

"Only problem is the computer system is inside." He looked across the street.

"Ok. Come with me." She told him.

Melissa turned then walked across the street with the young guy behind her.

They walked past the burnt out wrecks and into the shop.

Inside it was warm. The young guy stepped behind the counter to retrieve a set of keys. Melissa stepped behind him and saw the till screen flashing a large red sign.

"What's that?" She asked.

The guy looked at the screen.

"I hit the emergency shut off. Stops the pumps from working if the nozzle is lifted and closes the vents, effectively sealing the tanks."

Melissa nodded; she was impressed with his cool head and quick thinking under extreme stress.

She pointed at his arm and asked.

"Did you do that outside?"

The guy nodded and flushed a little.

"I slipped on the mat as I ran out to help. The concrete tore the skin up pretty well." He said as he touched it gingerly.

Melissa smiled again, amazed by his selfless act.

"Ok, show me the system, what's your name by the way?"

"Mark." He offered.

Melissa stuck her hand out, Mark shook it.

"I'm detective Melissa Cross. OK Mark, let's have a look at the footage."

Mark opened the manager's door then stepped into the cramped office. Two desks sat opposite each other. Both held computers and were covered in paper. Mark pulled up a seat offering it to Melissa.

He rounded the desk to gather another seat for himself and sat next to her at the computer.

He moved the mouse then clicked on an icon of a camera.

"This will take us into the system but then I'll need a pass code to access the files." He told her.

Mark opened the system and the screen prompted him for a pass code.

Mark lifted the receiver next to the computer and dialled a number. After a short conversation Mark dropped the receiver back onto the cradle then pressed a sequence of numbers and letters into the bar.

He hit enter and the computer listed three files. Daily, weekly and monthly.

"How much can this hold?" Melissa asked.

Mark looked at her.

"More than is really necessary. The owner is a little paranoid, he likes to keep records of everything, hence the mess." He said indicating to the room around them.

Mark clicked on the daily folder and brought up the most recent footage. The image was slightly grainy but clear.

The time counter showed eight fifteen in the morning, the explosion had been around ten thirty.

Mark moved the clock close to that time without being prompted. Melissa pushed fractionally closer watching as people walked into the shop then brought items over the counter.

Then there was a lull in activity, as if someone had sealed the doors to stop people from entering.

Three minutes into the lull a man entered the shop. He stopped at one of the fridges, selected an orange juice then walked up to the counter. He kept his head down as he approached but Melissa thought she felt a twinge of familiarity.

It was at that moment the man at the counter looked up, directly into the camera.

"I know him." Melissa whispered. Mark turned to look at her.

"I'm sorry to hear that." Melissa glanced sideways at Mark and realised what she had said.

"Oh no, I mean I've seen him somewhere before. I don't know him personally." She reassured him.

 Mark nodded.

"Can we see the forecourt?" She asked, her American accent sounding soft.

Mark clicked on another folder. A scene of the forecourt appeared on the screen with the same time stamp, moments before the explosion.

The picture showed another car hard up to the car in front of it. Melissa could clearly see someone in the second car but his features were indiscernible.

The man from the previous shot, true to Mark's word, placed the nozzle into the tank and stood there waiting for it to finish.

The man removed the nozzle, hung the nozzle on the pump, replaced the filler cap then climbed into his car.

A few moments later there was a spectacularly bright flash that hurt her eyes as the car erupted in flames. A few moments later she could see Mark race outside. He slipped and fell grazing his arm; he picked up a fire extinguisher and sprinted towards the cars. He could clearly see someone inside the first car but the intense heat prevented him from getting any closer.

"Can I get a copy of the picture in the shop please?" She asked.

"Sure, what's your email address, I'll send it straight to you?"

Melissa told him the address as Mark typed it out then sent it into the ether.

"Excellent, thanks for your help Mark. Take care of that arm." She said as she stood up.

Melissa headed for the door and stepped out into the cold wind.

She walked close to the cars then slowly around them taking in every detail, looking for something that didn't fit the scene.

"Anything useful?" Nick asked as he walked up behind her.

She spun around to face him.

"Not really. The attendant didn't see anything. He said it all happened too fast." She told him.

Melissa continued around the cars looking for anything that she could use to identify who owned the cars.

She looked at the body in the front seat. The heat had been that intense and abrupt the eyeballs had exploded. She knew they could identify a body via dental records but Melissa had her doubts in this case.

Mark walked outside with a slip of paper and handed it to Melissa.

"What's this?" She asked.

"I looked at the footage again this time from another angle. I managed to get the registration number of the second car." He stated as he handed it over to her.

"Thanks Mark. This could help us identify a potential suspect." She said as she looked at the number.

Mark nodded then turned on his heel, pausing slightly at the grizzly sight of the charred remains. He shuddered and walked back into the shop.

They spent another hour at the site until the body was removed along with the cars. Melissa turned then walked back to the squad car with Nick in tow.

The drive back to Auckland was in silence.

CHAPTER 31

Dan dropped himself into the seat in front of his computer. He clicked on the current affairs channel and browsed the latest stories.

Some parent had narrowly avoided conviction for killing his six month old baby. Dan read the article and could feel it invoke a response, which he suspected was exactly what the reporter wanted.

Construction had finally begun on the Kopu Bridge. The council had finally deemed it necessary to make it a two lane bridge instead of a single lane choke point.

Dan had firsthand experience of the delays that bridge could cause. He had travelled to the Coromandel Peninsula during a holiday period and vowed to never do it again. He spent five hours sitting in traffic waiting for the jam to clear.

A car at a petrol station had exploded in Paeroa Township. The article didn't really reveal much but it said one person had died in the flames.

Police from Auckland had been called for some reason but it was not stated why. Dan clicked on the article to read the full story. There was an aerial shot of the station. It was still standing but there was the tell tale sign of a blackened scorched area near the road.

Dan closed the page then opened his e-mail account. There was one e-mail from someone he didn't recognise. The subject line was blank.

Dan copied the e-mail then deposited it in another area of the computer that was secure. He didn't want anything screwing with his system.

The e-mail was deleted from the account then he opened the saved version.

It contained only two lines.

'I'm sorry for your loss' then below it.

'You have my condolences.'

Dan frowned; the cryptic message sent a small ripple of concern up his spine.

He asked himself if someone had died that he knew but didn't know about it.

He instantly thought of his parents then snatched the receiver from the cradle. He put it back down and found himself lost.

He wanted to make sure but he didn't want to be seen as a fool for worrying.

Dan lifted the phone again then dialled his parents' number.

"Dad, its Dan." He said when the phone was answered.

"Oh hello son, how are things up there?" His father asked.

Dan knew straight away that there was nothing wrong with them.

"I was just checking in Dad. Wanted to make sure everything was alright." Dan told his father.

"Everything is fine here, why what's happened?" He asked.

"Ah nothing, nothing Dad, everything is all good here." Dan told him.

They talked for another five minutes until Dan told his father he had to go. He hung up the phone then read the e-mail again.

Dan picked up the phone again then dialled Emery's number. The line rang.

He hung the receiver back up after a minute of waiting. Dan thought nothing of it, but he wanted to find where the e-mail came from, he knew there wasn't a lot he couldn't find.

Dan started his *HideandSeek* program which he had upgraded, extending the parameters to computer users as well. He loaded the e-mail into the program then hit the start button. It would take some time for it to sort through the internet and find the address after it found the I.P. user.

He left the computer running and went to the kitchen to prepare dinner.

His wife, Roxie, was still at work and occasionally left the cooking to Dan. He didn't mind, he enjoyed it even though he wasnt very good at it.

He heard the computer chime from the kitchen. Normally it took longer to find someone and he wondered if it was telling him that no such address existed.

It didn't.

The address was that of an internet cafe located in the heart of Hamilton city. He wrote the address down and promised himself he would look into it tomorrow.

Chapter 32

Melissa walked into the squad room. It was nearing dark and she was feeling tired. Winter in the city made it a sleepy town. She walked to her computer then opened her secure e-mail account.

She had spent time at the scene talking to people who told her they witnessed the explosion and surmised that the event had played out the way Mark had explained.

Only the night shift were on so most of the computer terminals had been shut down casting the squad room with an eerie glow from the street lights outside. The bright screen showed the e-mail Mark had sent her.

She pulled the email up then opened the attachment.

Melissa gazed at the face staring back at her, into his dark piercing eyes and knew she had seen him somewhere.

Then it hit her.

The hospital.

Hamilton hospital.

She felt a new wave of energy hit her, a piece of the puzzle had fallen into place, albeit a small piece. Melissa lifted the handset of the phone next to the computer and dialled the directory.

She asked to be put through to the hospital. When reception answered she asked for the morgue and was told that they were shut for the evening. They would be in at seven the following morning.

Melissa thanked the receptionist, she cut the call after letting her know she would be in touch early the next morning.

The drive to her apartment was short and quick. She stepped inside then flicked on a light. It instantly stung her eyes with a jab of pain shooting between her temples.

Melissa slapped the light off deciding to forego dinner. The encroaching advance of sleep was a battle she could not win.

Her head hit the pillow and instantly she was asleep.

Dan drove to Emery's the next morning. He had been awake for nearly three hours even though it was only seven o'clock in the morning. The traffic heading south was light. He made good time reaching Te Kauwhata.

Dan pulled into the entrance, the van crunching down the gravel driveway towards the house. He couldn't see any smoke from the fire or lights on in the kitchen. Dan pulled to a stop at the front of the house and climbed out.

The house was eerily quiet.

He walked to the front door and rapped his knuckles against the glass window. After waiting a moment he did it again, then a third time.

Dan frowned then turned and walked around to the rear of the property. The curtains were drawn over a dark room. Dan looked through a crack in the drapes but could see no one inside.

He knocked on the glass and called out but still there was no movement in the house.

Dan walked around to the front and removed his cell phone from the van. He dialled Emery's number. It began to ring.

Then Emery's phone began to chime from inside the house.

"Damn it." Dan whispered.

He climbed into the van then reversed to the end of the driveway. He headed through the small village and turned north, back towards home.

Melissa passed through the small township of Huntly on her way to Hamilton.

Traffic was light but by the time she arrived in Hamilton it was building. She navigated her way to the hospital and pulled into a parking lot for the public.

As she climbed from the car she made a mental note to ask Baker why he would give out details of an investigation, what did he have to gain from it and, more to the point, what exactly the hell he was thinking.

Melissa walked into the transit lounge and up to the receptionist. She asked to speak to someone from the morgue.

The receptionist nodded then lifted a receiver and dialled, what Melissa assumed, was the number at the morgue, she asked if the M.E. was available, nodded once then dropped the receiver back onto the cradle.

"The M.E. isnt in today, but Kathy will be here in a few minutes. She runs the morgue." The lady told her.

Melissa nodded and turned for the seats lined against the wall of the lounge.

Kathy arrived in two.

Melissa saw her coming and placed the magazine back on the table beside her then stood to meet Kathy.

"Detective Cross, nice to see you again. Is there something I can do for you?" Kathy asked.

"Yes. This person was involved in the explosion in Paeroa. I'm almost certain he was here but I dont know why." She asked as she held up an image taken from the security cameras in Paeroa.

Kathy looked at the photo and instantly recognised him as the guy who came to identify Amy's body.

"Yes, he came in here not long after you to ID Amy's body. Said he was an officer and had been told to confirm identification."

Melissa turned the photo in her hand and looked at it herself.

"He definitely isn't a police officer. He unfortunately perished in the fire. Did he say what his name was?" Melissa asked.

Kathy shook her head.

"No sorry he didn't, something did seem a bit off about him. We have only just received the body but have not been through the autopsy, so no formal ID yet sorry. "

Melissa nodded then asked.

"Do you have a card so I could get in touch with you if the need arises?"

Kathy turned then stepped towards the reception desk and snatched a card from a holder full of off white cards with a logo embossed into it.

She handed it to Melissa.

"My direct dial number is on there if you need it."

Melissa handed her a card and said if anything new came up then for her to call her. Kathy looked at the card then put it in her pocket. Melissa thanked her then turned for the parking building.

CHAPTER 33

The assassin walked through the streets of Tauranga. His target moved in front of him, slowly swaying from side to side. The client had made contact via an associate. Someone he liked to keep at arms length.

The assassin knew how to be quiet, he knew how to handle delicate situations. His time in the legion had taught him everything he needed to know, plus a whole lot more.

He excelled at eliminating people while making it look like an accident. Making the accident happen while he was not there was an ability that took him years to master. The assassin could read a scene and know all its various conclusions in an instant. He knew how to manipulate a subject, an area, anything he needed to get his desired outcome.

The explosion at the petrol station, which had been executed according to plan, was a testament to that.

The assassin had scheduled for this person to drown; the client had been very specific. She didn't want the body to be found, ever.

So he had purchased a boat, only a small one, which he had moored where there were few pedestrians and even less during the night. The assassin had watched the subject for two weeks straight and found he was a creature of habit, which made his life a lot easier.

As long as the man stuck to his usual patterns, the assassin wouldn't have any problem dispatching him.

This also made him wary.

The assassin knew from bitter and painful experience that anything could happen. The team he was a part of had walked into an ambush. He and one other had survived while the remainder of the team had perished in the fire fight.

Now he always thought ahead, always made contingencies if plans went awry, but tonight he believed that there wouldn't be any cause for concern.

The assassin had hesitated at first. He didn't normally get involved in affairs of the heart.

He had broken one of his rules meeting with the client. Only briefly, but it was long enough for him to realise that he would have done the job for free.

The subject turned right on Devonport road then walked the short distance towards the waterfront. He turned right again to follow the road to the apartment building overlooking the harbour.

The assassin looked across the train tracks, he could see his small boat tied to one of the pontoons a few feet away from the rock wall edge. He removed a small but powerful stun gun from his pocket while quickening his pace. He didn't need to test the device, he knew it worked.

The man stopped at a door groping his pockets in search of his keys. The assassin watched as he fumbled and dropped them to the pavement. The man bent over to collect them and slammed his head into the glass door in front of him. He stood up abruptly, shook his head then bent back down to collect them. The assassin stepped up behind him then touched the probes to the back of the his neck.

He was unconscious before he hit the pavement.

The man groaned, he was face down covered by an old blanket. The assassin ignored him as the boat continued out past the mouth of the harbour into the rolling swell. He didn't like the water very much but he tolerated it when he had to.

He piloted the boat out ten nautical miles. It was along way out for a small craft which meant it would be more than deep enough. If he remembered correctly it was around thirty metres to the ocean floor.

During the voyage out the inert body began to move. The assassin put his boot on the man then shoved him back down. The man thrashed trying to roll over but the assassin held him firmly in place.

"Just stay down, it will all be over soon." He calmly told the man.

The man stopped moving.

"Where the hell am I?" The man yelled.

The assassin ignored him and kept the boat heading steadily out into the vast ocean.

"Answer me!" The man screamed.

The assassin took his boot off the man and stopped the small engine at the same time.

"We're here." The assassin called quietly.

The assassin removed the old blanket he had found lying in a dumpster from the man while standing over him.

"Do you have any idea why we are here?" The assassin asked.

His voice devoid of emotion.

The man struggled on the wooden deck trying to look up. It wouldn't have made any difference anyway. The night was as dark as pitch. Only stars twinkled in the night sky supplemented by the fragile light from the port reflecting off the surface of the swell. The man rolled over to look up at the dark figure, his face clouded in confusion.

"No, I have no idea why I am here." He squealed in a panicked voice.

The assassin could still hear the slur of cheap alcohol in his words, knew he wasn't going to get a straight answer out of him. He just nodded then set about preparing for what was to come.

The assassin picked up a bucket to drop it over the side filling it with water. The gunwale of the small boat leaned dangerously close as he drew the bucket out of the ocean back into the boat. It thumped down on the deck.

"What are you doing?" The man asked, panic rising higher in his voice.

The assassin stayed quiet as he took a small bag of quick setting cement from the back of the boat, he sliced the bag open then began to pour the contents into the water.

The assassin looked at the man and knew from the silence that he was putting the scene together in his head.

The man kicked out at the bucket but the assassin was too fast. His boot clamped down over the man's lower leg holding it firmly out of the way.

The assassin set about stirring the contents until he could feel the concrete beginning to set.

"You don't have to do this." The man pleaded.

The assassin looked down at him.

"Yes I do. You see what you did is, well, unforgivable." The assassin stated quietly.

It wasn't until now the man thought he heard a hint of an accent. It was a thought he should have had if he had meet the man in passing, but now the rational was being forced aside to make room for the sheer blind panic that was gripping him.

The assassin stirred the concrete into the water. Slowly but surely the mix began to thicken.

It was then he heard the noise.

It was more of a scream.

The howl of a turbine engine working hard. The assassin looked up and scanned the horizon. He could hear the helicopter getting closer but couldn't see it.

"What the hell is that?" The man asked him.

The assassin said nothing, just continued scanning the horizon.

It was loud now, very loud.

The assassin could distinctly make out the hum of the tail rotor as the machine approached. He could tell just by the sound that it was a Hughes 500.

What model, he wasn't sure.

He stood up slowly scanning the surrounding darkness. The sound was almost deafening now. It had to be right on top of them.

The assassin felt the man beginning to struggle. He stepped forward carefully, his boot catching the man under the chin instantly knocking him unconscious. The assassin looked up to see a blur of faint red flash over head no higher than ten feet.

Instrument lights.

The helicopter was painted jet black; its registration letters taped a corresponding colour. The noise receded, the Doppler Effect telling him that they weren't turning so they hadn't seen them.

The assassin looked around the darkness, when he was satisfied that they would not be disturbed again he sat down next to the bucket then began pushing the stirring rod around.

The concrete was thickening nicely, it was almost time to add the final ingredient. He lifted the weighty bucket over to the man and placed it gently down by his knees, then lifted both his legs and placed them slowly into the concrete.

It took twenty minutes for the concrete to set solid. The assassin tapped the side of the bucket and found it unyielding. He took a knife then sliced the bucket from around the concrete block and set it to one side. He sat back waiting for the man to regain consciousness.

He didn't have to wait long.

The man groaned and slowly tried to sit up but he couldn't move. The assassin watched as he tried to kick his legs out but they were stuck fast. This time the assassin could see him clearly. He had a dull flashlight beam pointed at his face. Terror lined every feature. A small smile flicked across the assassins lips. He flicked the light off.

"Do you know why we are here?" He asked again.

The man was trembling; he could feel it, hear it in his voice.

"I have no goddamn idea man. What the hell are you doing?" He screamed.

The assassin shook his head then flashed the light back on the man's face and answered.

"Your wife. You hit your wife, that kind of behaviour really disgusts me. She wants you gone for good but she knows that you would only come back. Come back to haunt her, make her life a misery. I was asked to make sure you don't come back." The assassin told him matter-of-factly.

The man looked down at the concrete enveloping his lower legs.

"I promise, I'll leave her alone, I swear." The terror in his voice sounded pathetic, even to him.

The assassin turned the torch on the concrete block as if he hadn't heard a word he had just spoken.

"And this way, I know you won't." He whispered.

It was quiet. After the noise of the helicopter had receded to nothing, only the lapping of the waves could be heard against the hull of the boat.

"Its thirty metres to the ocean floor, give or take. The concrete is quick set, impossible to break without a chisel and hammer. Your lungs should be sufficient for around three minutes of air. But if you keep hyperventilating expect it to be a lot less."

The assassin clicked the light off then placed it back in his pack.

"Is there anything you want to say?" He asked politely.

The man struggled and fought but said nothing.

"Ok."

The assassin stood up abruptly rocking the boat precariously.

"Let's get this show on the road shall we." He stated.

He grabbed the concrete block then rolled it up the side of the small boat. The man tried to stop him but couldn't, he had no leverage. The concrete block reached the top of the gunwale as the man began to scream.

"Wait, wait, please wait." The man screamed.

The assassin stopped and turned to him.

"What?" He asked.

"I'll pay you double what she is paying you if you let me go." The man begged.

The assassin grinned in the darkness.

"Double of nothing is nothing." The assassin stated and with a final heave the block fell over the side.

The man screamed as he followed the block overboard into the inky dark ocean.

The assassin watched from the side of the boat as the scream was drowned out by the cold water.

He waved goodbye then set a course back towards the harbour inlet then eventually home.

Chapter 34

· ·

John stepped out of the cavern to begin the climb towards the top. It had been a week since the giant and he had convinced Amy that working for them was really the best option. Their drop was due to happen in a few days and he had a lot to prepare for.

Amy had been unwilling to work to her full capacity, like a child testing their limits with it's parents.

She had been persuaded otherwise.

John always maintained that he would release her after she had fulfilled her commitment to him.

And he meant it.

Although she was proving to be one of the most productive employees, he was beginning to have second thoughts.

John reached the top of the staircase then thumped on the door. He was slightly winded from the ascent but it passed before the door was opened.

The pilot stood in front of him holding a pistol.

"Proceeding to plan?" The pilot asked.

John just nodded as he stepped into the small room.

"We have a drop to make in a few days. Get everything ready, I want this to go smoothly." The pilot nodded then closed the door again.

The giant stepped out onto the cove and dug his toes into the sand. He turned and looked behind him at the small camping area. Two people milled about, lazing in the morning sun, cooking breakfast. The giant had told them he would go and catch dinner, so with his fishing rod and tackle box clutched in one hand he headed for some rocks he knew would be worthwhile.

On his belt he had clipped two radios. One could be tuned to air traffic frequencies, he had tuned it to Tauranga airport to listen for incoming and outgoing traffic, but mainly to keep tabs on the police helicopter.

The other was for communications around the island.

The giant set off around the cove, walking and climbing for a solid half an hour.

He reached a rock outcrop then sat down, his feet dangling over the edge. It was deep here, very deep, the giant had taken crayfish from the rocks below the surface.

He carefully tied a hook and a sinker to the line then baited it with some fresh squid and slowly lowered it to the water. It disappeared beneath the surface. The giant let the line out until he guessed he was a few feet from the ocean floor then clicked the brake in place.

He had been sitting like this for what seemed like hours. His eyes were starting to droop, he could feel sleep biting at the corners of his mind.

He shook his head vigorously reawakening his senses.

The island radio squawked, he turned to pick it up.

"Yeah." He said into the transmitter.

"Where are you?" Asked an electronic voice.

The giant could tell it was John.

"Fishing."

"We leave in two hours."

The giant dropped the radio into the tackle box and resumed waiting.

Amy looked up from her steel table. She had been surviving on four hours of sleep each night for the last five days. Her fingers were raw from the rough surfaces and handling the drugs. She felt sick; her appetite had disappeared along with any hope of escaping. There were two others kept with her, Ralph and Dirk.

From what she could tell they were here under the same circumstances. They had been kidnapped and forced into slavery. They were from another country, both were chemists. Amy could tell they had been here a long time, a lot longer than she had been, although it felt like eternity to her.

She watched them carefully.

Dirk could barely keep from falling over. A man with a gun was standing beside him at all times, prodding him when he began to faultier.

Ralph was the bigger of the two. He wore glasses with a broken lens.

From the other side of the cavern, Amy could tell Ralph enjoyed the science behind constructing the compounds for use, even if they did harm to other people. Every now and then though he would stop, placing both his hands on the table, a guard would step in landing a punch to his kidneys prompting him to work again.

The man named Rossi had visited the cavern often. Amy had kept track of when he came and went as accurately as she could but her mind was beginning to blur. It seemed to her that they were preparing for something to happen.

The armed men had made extra sure that Amy, Dirk and Ralph were pushed to their absolute limits. They weren't allowed a single moment to themselves. Even toilet breaks were regulated.

The familiar grinding of steel on steel echoed around the rock walls. Amy didn't bother to look up; she knew where it would be coming from.

"Amy." The ragged whisper called.

Amy looked towards the two boys standing on the other side of the cavern. Dirk was pointing in the opposite direction to the main door. Her head slowly swivelled around, her eyes widening at the sight.

The rock wall was disappearing, right before her eyes. It disappeared into a yawning darkness. Amy could feel how big it was; it felt larger than the cavern she had been confined to.

And then the breeze hit her. It rustled her tattered clothes, blowing white dust out off the plates in front of her. She covered her mouth, trying not to breathe it in. They had added an extra ingredient to the compounds boosting its strength ten fold.

Amy had inhaled some dust accidently on her second day and instantly become violently sick. The effects were still lingering three days later.

She backed away from the table, her hand still covering her mouth. The guard jammed the muzzle of his weapon into her back. She spun around as another breeze gently lifted dust from the benchtop.

Amy quickly dropped her hand.

"I can't work if I'm stoned." She yelled then quickly covered her mouth and nose again.

The guard eyed her then the settling dust cloud, it was coating everything. Amy could see it on the backs of her hands. It was in her hair and covering every surface with a sticky residue.

The guard's eyes darted around then he rushed off. He came back moments later carrying a dust mask and a damp cloth. He shoved them into her hands.

"Now get to work." He yelled at her.

Amy rolled her eyes at him then pulled the mask over her mouth and nose. She wiped her exposed skin to remove what she could then placed the damp cloth on the bench. She pretended to busy herself but her eyes were looking towards the darkness at the end of the cavern.

CHAPTER 35

Melissa charged into the squad room making a beeline straight for Baker's desk. She wheeled a spare chair around from an empty desk and planted it directly in front of his desk then dropped herself into it.

"What aren't you telling me Baker?" She asked with venom in her voice.

She folded her arms across her chest making her intention clear that she was not going anywhere until she had a straight answer.

Baker balked.

He wasn't prepared for her to go on the offensive. His jaw dropped open then closed again.

"Telling you about what?" He asked finally.

"Amy Tarrant, you know something and you aren't letting on." She whispered leaning forward.

Their exchange was getting noticed around the room.

"All I know is she was kidnapped." Baker told her.

Melissa's eyes bored holes into him. She could tell he was lying to her face.

"What, you know as much as I do, you were there." Baker pleaded.

Melissa rolled her eyes.

"Bullshit Baker. What aren't you telling me?" She spat as she thumped the desk.

Eyes turned to look at them both. Melissa ignored them, she wanted an answer.

Nick's eyes darted around the room looking for support but found none. Finally he relented.

"We have a hunch that she was kidnapped by Emery Blackstone." He whispered.

Melissa was confused.

"Who the hell is that?" She asked.

Baker lifted a photo out of a closed file. It was a photo of Emery, an older photo but it was him none the less. Baker handed it to her.

"This guy. He's a bad seed. A year ago he killed a few people but no one could lay it at his feet. A rapist murderer was operating in Auckland, we couldn't catch him."

Baker pulled another photo of a man in a cage. Both his knees had been shot out. Melissa gazed at the photo.

"That's the guy we were trying to catch. He kidnapped one of our detectives and used her as bait to lure Emery out. It didn't work as he had intended." Nick told her.

"So what, is Emery some kind of government agent?" Melissa asked.

Nick almost laughed at her then realised she was serious.

"No, he isn't, he's a vigilante." Baker replied.

"So, you're telling me that this guy did what the New Zealand police force couldn't." She stated, humour hinting in her voice.

Nick dropped his gaze to his desk, then looked back at her.

"Where does this guy live?" She asked.

Nick shrugged his shoulders.

"He's not listed anywhere. There was rumour he was living in Hamilton but that turned up empty. The only known lead we have is a guy called Daniel Marriott. He lives a half an hour south of here. But every time we ask him he says he hasn't heard from him in years."

"Do you have this guy's address?" Melissa asked.

Nick lifted a piece of paper from the file on his desk then handed it to her.

"It won't be of any use." He told her.

"We've already tried."

Melissa looked at the address then stood and walked for the door.

The drive took her more than three quarters of an hour to reach Dan's house in the Hunua Ranges. She drove up a long snaking gravel driveway then parked on a gravel turning area.

As she stepped from the car she looked down the range set into the hillside. Melissa could see a steel frame at the end of the strip. Carefully she looked around her immediate area. A side door opened and a man stepped out. He was dressed in jeans and a tee-shirt even though the temperature was in single digits. She walked up to him then pushed out her hand.

"Melissa Cross, Auckland Police." She stated as an introduction.

Dan looked at her then her hand and relented, slowly placing his hand in hers.

"You obviously know of me otherwise you wouldn't be here." Dan replied.

Melissa looked at him then at the ground and smiled.

"I'm looking for someone and I was told you might be able to help me find them." Melissa stated ignoring the dig.

"And who might that be?" Dan asked.

Melissa removed a photo and showed it to him. Dan looked at it then shook his head.

"No. Sorry. Can't help."

Melissa turned the photo over and feigned disappointment. She replaced it then removed another and turned it to Dan. It was the photo of Emery. Melissa watched carefully, she could tell a liar when she saw one.

Dan looked at the photo then at her.

"What do you want with him?" He asked.

"I was told that you might know where we can find him. We have reason to believe that he is responsible for the kidnapping of Amy Tarrant."

Dan eyed her closely.

"I can tell you right now he isn't." Dan told her flatly.

Melissa took the opening

"And what makes you say that?" She asked.

"He isn't in the country, is what makes me say that." Dan replied.

"Don't bullshit me Dan, Emery is in the country and if I'm correct, he was killed in a petrol station explosion two days ago."

Dan's eyes widened at the comment.

"You didn't know?" She asked more tenderly.

Dan's shoulders dropped.

"I'm sorry, I thought you knew. We were investigating the kidnapping of Amy Tarrant and an anonymous tip came to us saying to look for Emery. We were about to start with you when the explosion happened. He was the only person that perished." Melissa could see the news was a shock to him, she stayed quiet for a moment.

Dan looked up at her.

"We were looking for Amy as well. We think she was kidnapped by someone we know."

"Who is that?" She asked.

"Just someone we know that has a history for that sort of behaviour. And I'd rather deal with it myself." Dan told her, he wasn't in the mood for arguing.

Melissa was shaking her head.

"You can't do that Dan; you can't take the law into your own hands like that."

The fierceness that shot through Dan stunned Melissa. He stepped forward jabbing a finger in her face.

"Don't tell me what I can and cannot do." He snarled.

Melissa stood her ground.

"Let the police handle it." She said softly.

Dan relaxed a little.

"I'm going to find whoever did this." He told her.

"So stay out of my way."

"I can't let you do that Dan." She told him as Dan turned on his heel.

He stopped after a few paces then looked back over his shoulder.

"Are you going to stop me?" He asked.

Melissa said nothing.

"Didn't think so."

Chapter 36

The black 500's engine began to scream as the pilot thumbed the starter button. The rotors began to turn, soon disappearing into a clattering disk. The pilot watched all the gauges as the engine and transmission warmed up and the needles entered the green zone. He looked across at his passenger then thumbed the intercom button.

"Are you ready sir?" He asked.

John looked back at him nodding his reply. The pilot lifted the machine from the ground and rose vertically from the trees into open space. He kicked the machine around pointing it for Tauranga airport.

Thirty seconds into the flight the pilot touched the intercom button again.

"Sir, you have a phone call." The pilot touched a switch diverting the call to Rossi's headset.

"Yes." He answered.

"It's Martin. I've eliminated a threat to the business."

"Excellent." Rossi paused and before he could continue Martin cut in.

"Emery Blackstone is dead."

Rossi's eyes widened at the news.

"When did this happen?" He asked, panic rising in his voice.

"Three days ago. We hired someone to take care of him. He was getting too close to finding the girl."

"That was not suppose to happen." Rossi screamed down the microphone.

The pilot looked across at him then back out the bubble.

Rossi pinched the bridge of his nose; he could feel a headache coming on.

"Emery was supposed to be filling a shortfall we desperately need." Rossi explained.

"Now we aren't going to be able to meet the dead line. You've just killed us..." Then Rossi stopped, his eyes narrowed.

"What do you mean he was getting too close to finding the girl?"

"Someone hired him to find Amy. There is one other we need to take care of to cut any link between us." Martin explained.

Rossi's mind raced.

How could he have been so stupid he asked himself? He knew it was too good to be true.

Rossi thumbed the intercom button and told the pilot to turn around then continued talking to Martin.

"I want you to find this other link and remove them. Do you understand me Martin?" Rossi told him taking control of the situation.

"It's under control." Martin reassured him.

Rossi severed the connection as the helicopter flared and began to touch the ground.

The rotors had barely stopped turning when the giant came over the hill, a confused expression on his face.

Rossi climbed down from the cockpit and turned to face him.

"Problem?" The giant asked.

"Emery, he's dead. Apparently he isn't going to supply us what we need to fill the order, someone hired him to find our new recruit." Rossi told him flatly.

The giant gazed at him, his slate grey eyes dead of emotion. He turned on his heel and headed into the bush.

"I told you something like this would happen." The giant spat over his shoulder. Rossi ignored him as they continued through the bush.

"We need to get this order filled otherwise it's all of our necks on the line, do you understand?" Rossi told him after a moment.

The giant stopped then turned to face him, his hand reached out to grab him by the collar but was stopped by Rossi. His hand was filled with a pistol that was levelled at the giant's face.

"Just do as you're told." Rossi whispered.

The giant sneered at him then turned and kept walking into the forest. They reached the small wooden hut and stepped inside.

Rossi and the giant quickly made their way down the stairs to the cavern below.

The giant pushed the door open then stepped into the cavern. Rossi burst in behind him and pointed to a man. The guy strode over with an air of confidence and looked directly at Rossi.

"A complication has come up. We are going to be short unless you can keep this going for the next ninety six hours straight." Rossi pointed at the three chemists.

The man turned to look at his recruits.

"No problem." He stated as he turned back to Rossi.

Rossi turned and walked back up the stairs. A resounding thud echoed up the stairwell then the heavy boots of the giant. Rossi reached the top and saw the pilot waiting in the seat. A machine pistol across his lap.

"Let's go." Rossi said as he headed for the door.

"Back to the mainland?" The pilot asked.

"No, we are staying here until the pickup is made. We will take over and make sure everything runs smoothly. You head back, we will call if we need you." Rossi corrected him.

Dan drove to the address he had on the computer printout after he had traced the cryptic e-mail. It was an internet café as he had already identified.

He stepped from his car onto the rain sodden street then zipped his jacket all the way up. He started across the road, dodging cars and buses as he went.

He reached the other side then slipped into the internet café. It was half full, mostly teenagers playing the latest and greatest of online games. There were a few people just browsing the net.

Dan stepped to the counter. The guy behind it had long unkempt hair in dreads. A ring hung from his nose, he was dressed in dirty jeans and a colourful ski jacket. When he looked up, Dan instantly knew the guy was going to be no help. Still, he had to try.

"A message was sent to me from here. Do you have a log of all out going traffic?" Dan asked.

The guy looked up at him and shook his head.

"Not a chance mate; if we kept that kind of information we would need something a lot larger than this shop. Besides, it's illegal."

Dan looked hard at him.

"Someone sent me an e-mail from here and I want to find out who it was."

The guy placed his magazine on the desk in front of him.

"You could try searching the history; I doubt it will help though."

Dan turned to look at the bank of computers.

"Unless I know which computer he sent it from I could be here for months."

Dan turned and surveyed the small shop. A youngish guy was looking at him from the rear of the shop.

"How much to use one?" Dan asked.

"Couple of bucks." The guy told him.

Dan turned then walked onto the dull floor. He sat down at a computer and touched the mouse. The screen redrew into a scene of a meadow with a tree in its centre. A message popped up indicating he had mail.

"I haven't logged on yet." Dan mumbled to himself.

The mouse touched the icon, a small screen popped up.

It had an address on it. Dan knew the area. It was near Templeview in Hamilton.

He closed the browser and turned to slowly gaze at the occupants of the internet cafe again.

The man who had been staring at him had his head down, focusing intently on the screen in front of him. Dan stood up then walked from the cafe after he had paid the charge.

Dan stepped onto the street then crossed the pavement to his car.

He climbed in then pointed it west towards Templeview.

Chapter 37

It was dark. The assassin walked slowly up the street past the target house. He glanced once in its direction, just a slight shift of his head for a moment then carried on. It was a relatively quiet area so he had only seen a handful of pedestrians walking during his two hours of surveying, the rain had kept most people inside.

The assassin walked slowly up the street then stopped. He leaned forward a fraction, his chin on his hand as if he were studying something. It was purely for show if someone happened to see him, what he was looking for was a tail.

He straightened, then carried on crossing the road heading for an intersection.

A small car was parked hard to the kerb. From the distance he could only just make out the shadow sitting in the front passenger seat. He walked to the drivers door then carefully slipped a key into the lock and folded himself into the driver's seat.

'They're there." The assassin stated quietly.

The figure next to him only nodded.

"How do you want to do this?" He asked.

The figure turned to him and drew a pistol then cocked it. The assassin understood the game.

Slowly they stepped onto the street. They were both dressed in black, moving from shadow to shadow. They approached the house with the cracked driveway then disappeared into the darkness.

The figure stepped silently to the back door. He tried it but knew it would be locked. Cautiously he checked his watch. Two minutes to show time. Silently he set about picking the lock to the door.

There was a faint click after thirty seconds of movement, he carefully pushed the door open. The figure stood silently, slowly counting down the seconds.

His pistol was out, a suppressor screwed to the muzzle. There was a crash which was right on time, then all hell broke loose.

The blast inside the house sounded louder and more devastating than it really was. The assassin had smashed a window with a flash bang grenade then waited at the door for the fireworks to start. When the explosion hit he kicked the front door in and stepped into the darkness.

A door swung open at the end of the hallway. Someone stepped out dressed in boxer shorts holding an assault rifle. The man turned to see the assassin at the end of the hallway. He swung the rifle towards him then his head turned in the opposite direction mid swing. The guy's arms went limp and he fell to the floor.

Behind him, the figure dressed in black stood looking into the room. Two other bodies were in the process of climbing out of bed when he pointed the muzzle of the pistol through the doorway.

The assassin saw two spits of flame. The figure moved to the next room with practiced precision. The assassin pushed his way around the first door he came to and saw their target. He pressed a switch attached to his pistol and spoke quietly.

"Found him."

Moments later the figure dressed in black appeared at his side, he stuffed his pistol into his thigh holster then pulled a small black box from a pouch and jammed it into their target's ribs depressing a button.

A jolt of fifty thousand volts ripped through him instantly knocking him unconscious.

The assassin grabbed the target by his limp hand then began dragging him to the door. The figure in black drew his pistol and pushed around the corner in the opposite direction to cover their retreat. They both knew they were missing one person but they didn't have time to sit around and wait for him to show. The inert body thumped down the stairs one by one and onto the chipped concrete.

The assassin turned to the man behind him.

"Is everything in place?" he asked.

The figure just nodded then picked up the man's legs.

Martin awoke. He felt groggy, his entire left side was on fire. He lifted his head and opened his eyes wide but could see absolutely nothing. There was no light for his eyes to detect; he was in complete total darkness. Martin dropped his head back and realised he was sitting in a chair. He tried to raise his arms but couldn't move them. He wasn't paralysed; his arms were taped to the chair. His ankles had the same problem.

It was then his head began to pound unlike anything he had felt before. He carefully rolled his head from side to side and back and forward, trying to relieve the pain that was building between his temples.

A pained moan escaped his lips.

"Keep your mouth shut." A husky voice told him from the darkness.

Martin lurched forward in the seat, his eyes searching the gloom for the figure behind the voice.

"Who's there?" He asked, a hint of fear in his voice.

"Me. I'm here, that's all you need to know." The voice told him, deep and gravely.

There was silence in the darkness.

Martin listened but couldn't hear anything.

"You don't need to do this, I'm sure we can come to some arrangement." He pleaded with the darkness.

"All I want is information." The voice told him.

Martin gulped air. His mouth was dry, the headache was beginning to explode light spots in his eyes.

"What information, I don't know anything." He told the voice.

A light flicked on overhead. It was only a single bulb burning brightly but to Martin it had the intensity of a thousand suns.

His eyes jammed shut against the light.

"Where is she?" The voice asked again.

Martin forced his eyes open so he could scan the room.

It was small and very non-descript.

The floor was wooden as were the walls. He could only make out the ends of the room but there was no door in sight.

"I asked you where she is?" The voice boomed.

This time Martin sensed movement behind him. Martin tried to turn but couldn't move; he turned his head as far as he could to catch a glimpse of a table with something dark laying on it.

"I don't know what you are talking about." Martin said in a half laugh as he shook his head.

Martin heard the faint clink of steel on steel then the voice materialised in front of him. It was a figure dressed in black, from head to toe. In his gloved hand, Martin saw what had made the metallic sound.

"I'll ask you one last time Martin. Where did you take the her?" The figure asked.

Martin eyed the pair of lock wire pliers in the man's hands.

"What girl are you talking about?" Martin asked.

The man stepped forward slowly and lowered himself onto one knee. He held the pliers up for Martin to see.

"These are lock wire pliers, designed to twist stainless steel wire, locking bolts together on aircraft." The figure stated as he pulled the handle showing Martin the twist it produced.

Martin's mouth suddenly dried even more, his spread fingers clawing the arm of the chair. The man opened the jaw of the pliers and selected Martins index finger. Martin fought to keep his fingers tight in a fist but couldn't stop the man prying one from the tight ball.

The jaws of the pliers gripped his fingernail then the man clamped down on the handle squeezing the nail flat, the lock clicked into place. Martin could feel the pressure build.

The figure in black looked up one last time at Martin then down at the pliers again. He grabbed the round handle then violently yanked it down.

In one quick movement Martin's nail twisted and slipped from the nail bed.

He screamed in pain.

The man didn't stop; he set about prying another finger loose to begin crushing the nail with the pliers. Martin could feel sweat dripping down the side of his head, the man gripped the pliers quickly ripping them down. Martin felt his fingernail twist and suddenly lift from the bed below.

The nail slipped from his finger, again Martin screamed long and hard.

"Ok, ok. I'll tell you where she is." He cried in a panicked haze.

The figure looked at him.

"Who am I talking about?" He asked.

"Amy Tarrant." Martin spluttered.

"That's correct, now her location, or I start removing digits." The man told him as he clamped the jaws of the pliers shut on another finger nail.

Martin told the man everything. How he was hired by Rossi to kidnap her and when Emery started snooping around he turned to someone to get rid of him. The man listened quietly and didn't interrupt.

"Where did you and Rossi get your information?" The man with the pliers asked.

"Baker, a cop called Baker. He's dirty, Rossi has him in his pocket." Martin spat quickly.

Bolts of pain shot through his finger tips, up his arm to his head.

"And where is he located?" The man asked.

"Auckland, Manukau." Martin told him.

The man stood up, dropping the pliers to the floor as he did. Relief flooded through Martin.

"Did you get all that?" The man asked.

Martin heard a shuffle as a seat scraped against the floor, another identicle figure dressed in black stepped in front of him.

"Yeah, I got it." The second replied.

Martin looked from one to the other. His eyes widened at the sight of the pistol as the second figure drew it from a thigh holster then placed the silencer against Martin's forehead.

"Thanks for the help." The voice whispered.

Chapter 38

Dan drove to the address in Templeview. He had passed the city limits by two kilometres when he saw the address. The building was surrounded by old overgrown trees, their branches hanging almost to the ground. The entrance held a beaten and bent letterbox next to a sign saying the property was for sale. Dan read the address again then looked at the house.

"This can't be it." He mumbled to himself.

Carefully he climbed out of the van then looked up and down the road. He walked closer to the mailbox to read the number. The address was correct. He looked up the covered driveway. There were potholes filled with mud lying in two ruts disappearing under the trees.

And fresh tire tracks.

Dan walked slowly back then climbed into the van. He selected drive and drove slowly up the muddy track. It wound through the trees which dead ended at a house that was in dire need of repair.

Dan killed the engine then climbed out.

He spun a circle listening carefully. From where he stood he couldn't hear traffic on the main road.

He turned and surveyed the house more closely. Windows had been smashed and the garden was heavily overgrown. Dan stepped through the long grass and up to the front door. He looked down to see tire tracks ending at the landing. He stepped onto the small landing and pushed the front door open.

Inside the air smelt musty, he walked slowly into the long hallway. A room branched off either side of him. Dan turned to his right; it opened into a large dining room.

A large table surrounded by chairs sat in the exact centre, pictures of various scenes hung from the walls, some had holes in them, others were left untouched. There was an intricate chandelier hanging from a sturdy wooden beam overhead. Everything was covered in a fine layer of dust.

Dan turned and stepped back to the long hallway. He surveyed the ground carefully and saw footprints leading towards the rear of the house. Dan followed them. They turned right as the hallway opened out into another large living area. Not quite as large as the first.

Large sofas were placed around the edges of the room. A table sat in one corner with a small lamp at its centre. Behind one of the sofas another open door led to another room.

But Dan didn't have to look any further.

He had found what he was supposed to find.

In the centre of the room was a seat. In that seat was his relative, his hands taped down, a small red dot in the centre of his forehead.

Dan looked at him, not feeling anything.

He knew it would have happened sooner or later.

On the floor next to the chair were a box of matches and a bottle of clear liquid.

He stepped around a sofa and bent down to pick them up. He sniffed it carefully, it was alcohol. Taped to the side of the bottle was a note. Dan peeled it off and carefully read it.

He stood up to gaze at his deceased cousin, contempt on his face.

He squeezed the bottle hard spraying the corpse, soaking it through. Carefully, he stepped backwards laying a track of liquid as he paced to the front door.

Dan stepped outside spreading the remainder of the alcohol over the front door and frame then threw the bottle into the hallway. He dug into his pocket for the matches and removed one from the box. The flame flared on the small stick settling to a bright burn.

Without a second thought, Dan flicked the flame into the hallway stepping back off the small landing as the flames leapt through the house.

The flames only took moments to take hold of the dry timber.

The fire crews would be unable to stop the inferno; instead they would let it burn itself out as there was no danger to any other nearby structures. It would be after the flames had died that they would discover the burnt corpse at its centre.

Dan flicked his cell phone open as he drove through Huntly towards home. She answered on the third ring.

"Yes?"

"I have some information." Dan told Melissa.

"Ok, you can bring it…" Dan cut her off.

"No I'm not going there. If you want it, you come to me." He told her then slapped the phone shut.

Chapter 39

irk looked across the cavern at Amy. She was asleep on her feet. There had been some renewed urgency in the guard's demeanour. They hadn't been allowed to sleep for the last twenty four hours. They were barely fed and weren't allowed away from the tables for any reason.

Dirk stepped back, sniffed loudly then sneezed. He quickly found a machine gun jammed into the back of his neck. Dirk shuffled forward slowly and put his hands on the table. He looked across at Ralph then back at Amy.

Amy staggered forward to plant her hands on the table. She squeezed her eyes shut as she pinched the bridge of her nose. She felt dizzy and sick. Her stomach turned and her knees buckled. Amy collapsed to the floor.

"Amy!" Dirk yelled across the cavern.

He ran around the corner of his table and rushed to her side. As he crouched down he noticed boots standing next to him. Dirk looked up to see five rifle barrels pointed straight at his nose.

"Get back to work." One of the guards snapped.

Dirk looked down at Amy. Her head rolled to one side as she groaned. Dirk saw her body convulse as she vomited on the stone floor. Some of the guards recoiled in disgust.

"She's sick. You can't keep us down here like this, we're being poisoned." Dirk pleaded with them.

The guards looked at him then one said.

"You have five minutes to clean her up then get back to work."

Dirk looked down at her. He carefully picked her up and helped her to her feet, all the time feeling dizzy himself.

They staggered to a chair and he gently sat her in it. Her head hung forward over her shoulders; Dirk had to push her back so he could splash some water on her face. Amy's eyes fluttered open then closed again. Her throat worked as she swallowed back bile, her eyes opened again. She raised her hand to her head and groaned.

"Hey, are you ok?" Dirk asked.

Amy took a moment to focus on the voice in front of her.

A guard came rushing over to them.

"Hurry up, get back to work!" He yelled at them.

"She's too sick…." The guard cut him off with the muzzle of his pistol.

"NOW!" He screamed.

Dirk stood up lifting Amy with him. He carried her to the bench next to his and stood her at the table. He turned to Ralph.

"Go use her station. I'll keep an eye on her here." Ralph just nodded then walked to the vacant table to pick up where Amy had stopped.

Dirk turned to see a pair of machine gun wielding guards watching them closely. Dirk leaned close to Amy.

"Make it look like you are doing something." He whispered.

Amy turned to him still in a daze. He pointed to the guards behind them, she followed his finger.

Her eyes widened a little and she slowly turned back to the table in front of her.

Rossi stepped out of the cabin. It was set back in the undergrowth but it only took him twenty paces before his feet were in the soft white sand of the cove. Most mornings he would rise early to take a swim in the small cove. He waded into the water up to his waist then disappeared beneath the surface.

He used the time to think. He walked through the events of yesterday again.

He had placed too much trust in a person he barely knew.

He was going to have Emery rescue his operation.

As he swam, he mentally cursed himself.

How could he have been so stupid?

He surfaced to take a deep breath then began swimming for the edge of the cove.

He put that thought aside and focused on the current situation.

Emery was dead but the short fall would be met. He knew they could pull it off.

They had to.

There wasn't any time to do otherwise.

Rossi reached the edge of the cove where the rocks provided an amount of protection from the open sea. He stopped then began to tread water, looking out to sea towards the coast between the swells.

He turned and began to swim for the shoreline again. Rossi was a powerful swimmer, he knew he could make it.

As his arms fell to the water powering him along, he thought about the giant, he was beginning to be a problem.

And Rossi hated problems.

There was also the question of what to do with the three recruits when the shipment had been fulfilled.

He already knew the answer to that; there would be an extra number of weighted caskets for the vessel to dump overboard during the journey back.

He was convinced that the giant wouldn't be a problem but to be on the safe side he would have to take care of him himself.

Rossi reached the shore then ran up the soft sand. He felt cleansed, his thoughts in perspective.

As he pushed into his cabin to shower and dress, he stopped dead, the giant was sitting at the small table, leaning forward gazing at the floor, his fingers bunched together, a knife lying on the table beside him.

"Need a word." The giant stated.

Rossi stood in the doorway, seawater dripping on the concrete step.

"About what?" He asked.

Rossi calculated if he could sprint past the giant before he could move to retrieve his pistol, which, inconveniently, was in the next room. The giant eyed Rossi standing in the doorway.

"There has been an interesting development over there." The giant said indicating with a nod towards the main land.

Rossi took a step inside to pick up a handy towel then began wiping the water from his skin. He remained quiet, waiting for the giant to continue.

"It seems we have attracted the attention of the police. Your source, the cop, Baker, tells me that a detective is trying to track down the girl. Oh and what's more, is that she isn't just any kind of detective, she's DEA." The giant told him with a flick of his hands.

Rossi almost laughed aloud.

"You can't be serious?"

The giant just shook his head.

"This is getting too dangerous; you have to tell them that we can't make the deadline. We need to shut the line for a while to let things cool down." The giant told him.

"I can't do that; and you know it. If we stop now we will all wind up fish food." Rossi countered.

The giant looked down at the floor between his feet. Rossi continued to wipe at the sticky seawater and was caught completely off guard when the giant exploded from the seat, the knife in his hand.

The giant stepped across the floor in two huge steps jamming the razor sharp blade to Rossi's throat.

"You will shut it down now." The giant whispered.

Rossi could feel the pressure increase against his throat. Up this close he realised how powerful the acrid stink of the giant's sweat was. It filled his nostrils choking him.

He nodded gently making calming gestures with his hands, afraid to speak should the blade slit his throat. The giant backed away slowly, lowering the blade.

Rossi looked at him as his hand involuntarily touched his throat.

"All I can do is try. You know that. These are not the type of people we can just back out on at a whim. These are very serious, very dangerous people." Rossi reasoned.

The giant shot Rossi a hard stare and slammed the blade into the table top where it dug into the hard wood a quarter of an inch.

"Then what the hell should we do about this DEA agent?" The giant yelled.

Rossi wrapped a towel around his waste.

"Easy, eliminate her." Rossi said simply.

The giant nodded.

He cast a glance at the rising sun over the ocean then yanked the blade from the table top and gazed hard at Rossi.

"That is going to be easier said than done." The giant told Rossi as he headed for the door.

Rossi turned to watch the steroid built monster go. He closed and locked the door quietly then took a shower; keeping his pistol within easy reach should the giant change his mind.

Chapter 40

Melissa drove at the posted speed limit all the way to Dan's house. She wanted to know what he was talking about and was prepared to bend to his rules to find out.

She bumped over the metal cattle stop steering her way down the gravel driveway then pulled to a stop beside the house and stepped from the car. She closed the door and spun a slow circle.

The place was quiet, not country quiet but the type of quiet a house takes on when no one is home. Her shoulders slumped; Melissa hated waiting for anyone or anything. She was driven to get things done, now, once she had latched onto something she wouldn't stop until it was concluded.

Melissa slouched against her car, her impatience growing by the minute. Twenty minutes later as her temper was getting the better of her, she heard the rattle of the steel cattle stop and spun to see a van slowly making its way towards the house. She stood still as the van pulled to a stop next to her car, Dan climbed out.

"I wasn't expecting you to show." Dan told her.

Melissa dispensed with the pleasantries.

"What information do you have for me?" She asked.

Dan looked down the range at the steel frame, half a ping pong ball floated in the breeze.

"I know who kidnapped Amy." He told her.

Melissa didn't portray any emotion. She remained quiet waiting for Dan to continue.

"A relative of mine had taken her, killing her flatmate in the process." Dan told her.

"Yours?" She asked not bothering to hide her surprise.

Dan nodded in disgust.

"Do you know where he has taken her?" Melissa asked him.

Dan shook his head.

"No, I don't, but I know one person who might." He told her.

"Who?"

"Emery."

Dan and Melissa drove towards Hamilton.

"Emery is dead." Melissa told him.

Dan just looked at her.

"Get off here." He said as he pointed at the Te Kauwhata turn off.

Melissa followed the road and bumped over the train tracks into the small village. Dan guided her to Emery's house. She drove down a long metal driveway then pulled to a stop in front of a low lying dark brick house. Dan stepped out of the car and walked into the garage. Melissa followed, watching carefully as he searched for a key.

"We aren't going to break into here." She told him.

Dan stopped for a moment to stare at her then carried on searching. He couldn't find the hidden key.

"Damn he must have taken it."

"Taken what?" She asked.

"His spare key. He usually leaves it somewhere. Only problem is he moves it every other day, making it impossible to find."

Dan reached into his coat pocket removing a small red pouch. He carefully selected two steel lock picks then pushed them into the lock on the sliding door.

"I'm not seeing this." Melissa stated shaking her head as she turned away.

Dan looked at her then carried on. It took him two minutes to defeat the lock during which time Melissa told him about all the laws they were breaking by just being there.

Dan slid the door open and stepped inside. He punched in a code to the alarm and waited for the light to turn green.

They both stepped into the hallway then glanced around the living room and dining room area. Dan turned to walk down the short hallway towards the concrete strong room. Standing in front of a discrete key pad he pressed in a combination. There was a faint electronic click and the door shucked open. They stepped into a small but full room. Shelves lined the walls stacked with everything from ammunition to components to parts. Dan stepped up to another door then pulled it open to reveal the gun cabinet. He peered inside and shook his head, cursing quietly.

"What's wrong?" Melissa asked.

"It's gone." Dan told her, still looking into the cabinet.

He saw most of the ammunition was missing as well.

"What is missing Dan?" Melissa asked, frustrated with the cryptic clues.

Dan turned to her.

"His target rifle. He spent years building it, its not here."

"We searched the car. There wasn't any evidence of any weapons of any kind at all. The body was charred beyond recognition, identification is going to have to be done the hard way." Melissa told him.

Dan nodded.

He reached into the cabinet selecting a Beretta M9A3 and a surppressor then shoved them both into a bag. He dropped two boxes of ammunition in the bag then zipped it up.

"I hope you have a licence to handle that?" Melissa cautioned.

Dan shot her a grin shaking his head.

They retraced their steps then locked the place back up.

In the car on the way to Hamilton, Dan turned to Melissa.

"He got what he deserved you know."

Who?" She asked.

"If you've read Emery's file, then you know who I'm talking about."

"Jacob." He stated glancing at her.

"He was only ever going to be stopped by a bullet." He continued.

Melissa cast a sideways glance at him then focused back on the road as she spoke.

"That isn't justice, that's murder. Emery is just as bad as the people he says he stops."

"That maybe true, but if he didn't, I, along with numerous other people would be dead." Dan said quietly.

Melissa glanced at him again.

"Someone came to see me, to tell me they were after him. I told this to Emery, he told me not to worry, said they weren't going to kill him."

"Who was going to kill him?" Melissa asked.

"My relative, the same person that kidnapped Amy." Melissa cocked her head to one side; the information didn't make sense to her.

"What did he do?" She asked.

"He was heavily involved in the gangs. From time to time he would be hired to eliminate people. He wouldn't actually do the job himself; he didn't have the stomach for it, instead he would find someone else to do it. Be the middle man." Dan explained to her.

They drove in silence for the rest of the journey to Hamilton. Melissa phoned ahead to request that Kathy meet them at the morgue. They wanted to see Emery's charred remains.

Chapter 41

Rossi and the giant descended the stairs to the cavern again. The delivery date was drawing close. The giant opened the door and they stepped into the toxic atmosphere. Instantly Rossi's senses were assaulted by the cutting fumes being emitted from the ingredients used to process the drugs. He walked up to the man who was overseeing the manufacturing then tapped him on the shoulder. The man turned to Rossi to look at him with dead dark eyes.

"Are we on schedule?" Rossi asked.

The man nodded but did not answer. Rossi cast a glance at the three recruits standing at the tables. He was frustrated to see that their movements were lethargic. One of the guys dropped something glass on the floor which elicited a rifle butt to the back of his head followed by barrage of abuse. Rossi could feel a slight tinge of panic building in the pit of his gut.

He stifled it and turned towards the door. The giant followed then slammed the door behind them locking everyone in the cavern again.

They crested the stairs and exited the small cabin into the sparse forest. Rossi turned to the giant.

"I want you to find that DEA agent and bring her back here."

The giant nodded then disappeared into the undergrowth, Rossi followed.

It took them half an hour to reach the camp at the cove. The giant didn't stop; he walked straight into the water up to his waist then onto the waiting boat, signalling the Captain to fire the engines.

The giant vanished below deck as Rossi stood amongst the trees watching the boat disappear behind the rocks.

The Captain pushed the throttles home causing the boat to rocket forward, driving its hull through the swell like a knife. The door to the cabin swung open and one of the deck hands stepped inside.

"The fish are running." He stated.

The giant looked up at him.

"What kind?" He asked.

"Marlin, Tuna, decent sized snapper."

The giant stood and flexed the huge muscles of his shoulders then headed for the door.

Kathy stepped through the door to the morgue with a vile of blood and paperwork identifying who it belonged to. She walked the short distance to the main building then climbed the stairs towards the red hall. She had walked thirty metres when she heard fast footsteps behind her. She turned to see a familiar face coming towards her.

"Melissa. I didn't think you would be here so soon." Kathy stated.

She looked behind her to see Dan shuffling his feet uncomfortably.

Melissa turned then stepped to one side.

"This is Dan. He's here to identify Emery's body." Melissa stated as an introduction.

Kathy nodded.

"Ok, I have to drop this to the lab, then I'll be right back." She stated, holding up the small vile of blood.

Melissa nodded and Kathy spun on her heel. She walked off disappearing around a corner.

Melissa turned to Dan.

"How do you know it isn't Emery in there?" She asked.

Dan shrugged his shoulders.

"Hunch." He replied.

They waited in silence for Kathy to return. Melissa's foot began tapping impatiently on the linoleum. Dan looked at her then the ground. Her foot stopped and she glanced at him.

"What?" She asked.

Dan shook his head pasting a confused look on his face that slowly turned to a grin. Dan broke his gaze away to watch Kathy walking down the hallway towards them. She stopped and addressed them both as she held up a thin folder.

"These are the results of the blood tests that were conducted. They will tell us the time of death, how he died and what he had in his blood, if anything, at the time of death." Kathy pushed past them before they could ask questions and led them both to the morgue.

She pushed the door open and they were instantly assaulted by the smell of powerful disinfectant. Kathy carried on, undeterred. She pushed through another set of doors into the rear of the building.

Melissa then Dan followed.

A man in a lab coat was at a table, writing in a folder. He looked up and saw Kathy walking towards him.

"You get that blood to the lab?" He asked.

Kathy nodded, her dark hair bobbing up and down. She placed the thin folder on the bench in front of him.

"Toxicology report for the burnt body." Kathy told him.

The man in the coat lifted the folder and removed a single slip of paper. He began reading through it and blew out an impressed whistle.

"What?" Dan asked.

The lab coat looked up at him.

"Did this guy do drugs?"

"Not likely. Emery liked to keep himself straight. He had the odd beer every now and then but nothing else." Dan told him.

The lab coat looked at him.

"This guy has been pumped so full of this new synthetic drug its scary."

Kathy walked around the edge of the desk to read the report.

Dan watched her lips part as she read the information. He knew right away that it wasn't Emery they had in here, locked in a steel drawer.

"It's not him." Dan said to Melissa.

The man in the lab coat stood then walked towards a bank of steel covers and selected a number. He slid the lock back then pulled the draw open.

The body was covered in a white sheet.

Melissa looked down, a scorched hand protruding from beneath the cloth.

She felt a shudder tingle her spine.

The lab coat gathered a corner of the sheet and slowly lifted it back to reveal what lay beneath. The body was burnt beyond recognition.

Dan looked carefully.

Two dark holes where the eyes were supposed to be looked back at him.

"What happened to his eyes?" He asked.

Kathy looked at him; she knew the answer but didn't want to say the words.

"They burst in the heat." The man in the lab coat told him.

Dan could feel his stomach turn but he forced himself to stay where he was.

Melissa turned to him.

"Are there any identifying marks, any tattoos he may have shown you?" She asked.

Dan just shook his head.

"Not that I can think of."

The lab coat picked up the file again and continued reading the sheet.

"Ok, here we go, Emery's blood type is listed as ORH positive. The blood from the body as AB negative. They don't match." He stated to the group.

Melissa and Dan both looked at him. It was Melissa who spoke first.

"Where did you get that information from?" She asked.

There had been nothing stated on the police file, she knew from experience that information garnished from those particular files was very extensive.

The doctor looked at the sheet. He read it again but couldn't find a source for the information. He shook his head then looked at Melissa.

"It doesn't say." He told her.

Melissa frowned, information like that didn't just materialise out of thin air.

"May I?" She asked holding out her hand.

The doctor gave her the leaf of paper, Melissa studied it closely. There was information for Emery along side the information garnished from the corpse.

None of it matched.

"This doesn't make sense. If this isn't Emery, then who is it?" Melissa asked.

The group looked at each other until Dan broke the silence.

"I think we should be asking, if this isn't Emery, then where is he now?"

Chapter 42

The assassin had tailed them. He knew where they were going and what they were going to do. He kept his distance parking a block away as they pulled into the parking lot. The assassin stepped from the car then walked slowly down the sidewalk.

As he approached the large complex, he stopped to survey the surrounding area. To any person simply observing him it would look like he was taking in the scenery.

He reached into his pocket quickly; his phone had insistently begun calling him.

"Yes." He answered.

"Are they there?" The voice asked.

"Yes." The assassin replied.

"Ok you know what to do." The voice told him then the line was severed.

The assassin slipped the phone back into a hidden pocket and remained standing on the sidewalk.

He wouldn't have to wait long.

The giant called ahead to the gang house telling them he was on his way. The leader's voice sounded shaky. He told the giant, two people had come in during the night kidnapping Martin.

The giant sighed.

"I don't care where he is or what has happened to him. All I want you to do is find that agent from the city. I'll give fifty grand to whoever finds her first." The giant stated.

This brought silence. The giant used the opportunity to carry on.

"And that's ALL I want, for her to be found. I'm a half hour out; I suggest you get moving." The giant told him, then clicked the phone shut.

He placed it on the passenger seat and drove for five minutes. He picked the phone up again then dialled a number.

Baker answered.

"Rossi is extremely pissed off at the moment." The giant told him.

Baker gulped and swallowed loud enough for the giant to hear it.

"He wants to know where the DEA agent is." The giant told him.

Baker paused for a few seconds before he answered.

"She's in Hamilton, identifying Emery's corpse." Baker rasped.

"Where was the body taken?" The giant asked.

"The main hospital morgue." Baker told him.

The giant clicked the phone closed not bothering to reply.

He pressed his foot down harder breaking the posted speed limit to Hamilton.

Dan and Melissa stepped into the morning sun. Winter was drawing to a close. The days were beginning to lengthen and warm up.

Melissa turned to Dan, her blonde hair shining in the sunlight.

"Do you have any idea why he would fake his death?" Melissa asked.

Dan shook his head as he looked around the car park. People were walking in the sunshine, holding hands and making the most of the weather before it turned bad again.

"I've been asking myself that question since you told me he was dead." He stated.

He sighed then looked down at the cracked pavement.

"He was working on a drug dealer in Tauranga. He thought this guy might be something big, turns out he was right. He was about to start gathering evidence to bring against him then I turn up to tell him about Amy being kidnapped." Dan told Melissa.

Melissa nodded but didn't say anything.

"We went to take a look at her flat and found a rag that had been soaked in Halothane. Then we found the other body and called the cops. I had an idea at that point who had taken her so we followed the lead. It dead ended. We were told she was lying in the morgue at the hospital." Dan told her pointing over her shoulder.

"He didn't tell me because the guy who took her was my cousin." He continued. Melissa looked at him.

"What do you mean was?" She asked.

Dan sighed and looked across the parking lot. A hundred metres away a man was watching them. He locked eyes with him before he answered.

"I found him in an old house that was for sale at Templeview, tied to a chair with a bullet hole in his forehead." He told her.

"I can only guess as to what they asked him." Dan said looking back at her.

Melissa nodded as she glanced at her shoes, she was trying to put the pieces of the puzzle together but they just wouldnt fit.

Dan looked at her, he was about to say something he remembered when a car pulled up next to them and a man climbed out of the driver's seat. The man walked around the rear of the car to open the passenger door next to Melissa. She had to step to one side to allow room for this to happen.

Dan watched it all unfold in slow motion. He looked across the parking lot at the man who had been watching them.

He was now running towards them, running fast. Dan looked back at the man just as his fist connected with his cheek.

Dan went down hard.

Melissa stood stone still, wondering what had just taken place.

"This was almost too easy." The man said.

He grabbed her neck in a vice like grip then threw her into the car as if she were a rag doll. Her head hit the driver's door and she yelped in pain. The giant slammed the door shut, locked it, then quickly ran for the driver's door and wrenched it open. He grabbed a handful of hair and shoved the cop back into the passenger seat.

There was a low cough, a split second later the driver's window exploded in a shower of glass. The giant looked across the car park to see a man running at him with a pistol in his hand.

As the engine caught, he gunned it across the car park skidding out onto the road. The man fired again shattering the rear windscreen of the car, then watched them disappear.

He holstered the pistol in frustration then bent down to collect the spent brass. It fell into his pocket with a light ding against the first expended round. He looked down at the inert body of Dan.

"Get up; this is going to get serious."

The man turned and walked across the car park disappearing into a crowd of people.

Kathy ran to the car park. She had seen the whole scene unfold, panic began to rise in her stomach at the sight of Dan lying on the ground not moving. She dropped to her knees and checked for a pulse, it was there, rapid and strong. Kathy smacked his shoulder.

"Dan, wake up." She called urgently.

His eyes flickered open and he lifted his hand to his cheek.

"Oh man, that hurt." He groaned as he gingerly touched the swelling.

Kathy helped him sit up.

"What happened?" She asked.

Dan shook his head and felt a jolt of pain race through his temples. He groaned and pressed his temples gently.

"We got jumped by someone, someone big." Dan mumbled as he spat out a glob of blood.

"Someone with one hell of a punch." He continued.

Kathy looked around at the gathering crowd.

"Maybe you should come in and get yourself checked out." Kathy told him helping him to his feet.

He shook his head.

"No I can't. I have to find Emery." He told her.

"Emery can wait. You won't be any good to him if you slip into a coma." She insisted.

Kathy wasn't going to take no for an answer. She took his hand then began walking him towards the entrance.

Dan stopped her.

"I'm fine, really." He said as he touched his cheek.

Kathy looked at him with an expression that said she had heard it all before.

"It won't take long." She told him.

Dan was about to reply when he felt his stomach turn. He bent forward and threw up barely missing her.

Kathy grasped his hand tighter and dragged him towards the hospital.

Chapter 43

Melissa awoke to the sound of a car engine being pushed. Her eyes flicked open but she didn't move.

"I was wondering when you were going to wake up." The giant told her.

Melissa looked up; her head was jammed against the window. She tried to move her hands but found them bound together with tape. Her eyes widened when she realised she was completely immobile. Her neck was taped to the head rest, her feet were bound.

"Now, are you going to behave?" The giant asked.

Melissa's eyes darted to him. She nodded as much as the tape would allow. The giant grinned and focused back on the road.

"Cause I would hate to have to hurt you." The giant told her as he looked through the glass.

Melissa stayed quiet trying to keep herself calm. She tried freeing her wrists again but couldn't find any purchase.

The giant looked across at her and grinned.

"We know who you are Melissa Cross. We know you're DEA. We know you are here for us Melissa. Thanks to our informant, we have been on to you all along." The giant smiled at her.

Melissa looked away.

She focused on the dash board before she asked her question.

"Who told you?" She asked quietly.

"You know him; well you should know, you work with him." The giant smiled again.

"Baker." She whispered, wanting to hear the name out loud.

"We have a delivery in thirty six hours, and we need to make it. You were causing major problems for us so it was decided that we could best keep an eye on you if you were a guest of ours." The giant told her.

Melissa looked sideways at him.

She didn't know what this monster was capable of so she stayed quiet for the remainder of the trip.

The assassin climbed into his car then pulled out of the parking space. He dialled a number and waited for a response.

"Yes." The voice asked.

"Silver ford. It's heading across town, going east from the hospital." The assassin told the voice.

There was silence.

"Ok." The line was severed.

The assassin blew through a red light chasing the car. It would take him at least twenty minutes to get across town if he caught all the lights right.

Which he didn't.

The first set of lights he came to fell red. He stopped and thumped the wheel in frustration.

He couldn't afford to be pulled over for a stupid traffic violation.

The light turned green then he gunned the car across the intersection and down to the bridge crossing the Waikato River. His cell phone chimed as he hit the eighty zone. He collected it from the passenger seat flipping it open.

"I have them heading south east on State Highway One. I'll be in touch." The line severed.

The assassin had to hand it to him. He knew how to track people.

He travelled for three quarters of an hour. He eyed the gas gauge and estimated he had at least another three hours worth of fuel. The assassin quickly calculated how far he could drive before he had to refuel.

It wasn't far.

He reached an intersection that branched the main highway, splitting the road south and east. He pulled to the side of the road. The assassin's phone chirped and he answered it before it had finished the first tone.

"Yes."

"They are heading for Tauranga."

The assassin nodded.

"You think this could be Rossi?" He asked.

"I'm betting on it." The voice stated then the phone clicked off.

He pulled the car to the left and headed east.

Dan sat on a hospital bed thinking as a nurse fussed around him. His cheek had turned purple which was slowly creeping to his eye.

The colour was turning darker and darker by the minute reflecting his mood.

He glanced up at Kathy who was across the room from him.

"You're lucky he only hit you once. The guy looked like he was popping steroids, all brawn and no brains." She told him.

Dan rolled his eyes but said nothing. The nurse finished by putting three butterfly stitches on his cheek under his right eye. He pushed himself off the high bed and landed lightly on his feet. The headache had subsided partially.

Kathy walked up to him.

"I think you should go home and rest." She told him.

Dan shook his head.

"You know I'm not going to do that." He told her.

She nodded, she knew he wouldn't. Slowly she turned for the door. At the door she turned back and looked over her shoulder.

"Be careful." She said, then she was gone.

Dan walked out into the sunshine then over to the parking lot. Police cars surrounded the area; he walked up to the crime scene tape and studied the scattered glass on the ground. He vaguely remembered what the man had said to him before Kathy had taken him into the hospital. Dan removed his cell phone from a pocket to glance at the screen. The time said it was drawing close to midday.

Just then the phone began to ring.

Dan gazed at the number on the screen. It wasn't one he was familiar with. Tentatively, he pressed the answer button.

"Yes." He asked.

"Tauranga port, two hours." Then the line was cut.

He looked at the phone as if it were something foreign, something he had never seen before.

Dan shoved the phone into a pocket and looked across the street; Melissa's squad car was still parked at the curb. He crossed the street thinking he would try the door handle. He had no reason to believe it would be unlocked but he tried anyway.

Locked.

Dan pulled his set of steel lock picks then jammed two into the door lock. The lock clicked up after a minute of manipulating. He climbed into the driver's seat to start searching for the ignition wires.

Inside of fifteen minutes the hospital had disappeared in the rear-view mirror and he had nearly cleared the city limits.

Chapter 44

The giant turned onto route PJK, the road that would lead him to the wharf.

The smell of the salt air was drifting in through the smashed window. Traffic around the port city was light. He navigated his way through town then out to the end of the peninsular towards the marina. The yacht club was closed up tight with only two cars parked at the far end.

The giant pulled into a vacant spot halfway along the edge of the marina. He cut the engine then sat there looking at the millions of dollars worth of boats moored at the wharf.

"Beautiful, isn't it?" He asked Melissa.

She didn't reply, only sat there gazing out the window, quietly working at the tape around her wrists which had started to cut into her skin.

The giant looked across at her.

"Well, we best be off then." He told her as he opened the door.

"Where are you taking me?" She asked.

The giant didn't answer, only pointed out to the wide ocean.

He climbed out, hauling a coat off the rear seat as he stepped out. The giant then walked to the passenger door and swung it open. He knelt down beside her and removed a small knife from his pocket. The blade flicked open, four inches of gleaming steel held menacingly in the giant's hand.

"Now, we aren't going to have any problems are we, Melissa?" He asked slowly as the blade glided across the skin of her throat.

Her throat worked as the edge pressed against her skin.

Carefully she shook her head.

She knew at this moment it would be useless for her to try anything. She had spent the entire two hour trip running through the odds.

He had at least two hundred pounds on her. Her hands and ankles were tied and she was restrained to the seat.

She knew it was hopeless.

The giant's hand twitched and she felt the pressure release from around her throat. He ripped it roughly from her skin then reached down to slip the knife through the tape securing her ankles. The giant quickly brought the knife to her throat again.

"Remember, don't try anything." He whispered.

He snapped the blade back into the handle then slipped it into a pocket.

The giant grabbed Melissa by the elbow lifting her from the car. He slammed the door, not bothering to lock it, then draped the coat over her wrists and quickly led her towards the marina steps.

They stepped through the gate and walked swiftly towards a launch at the end of the pier.

"The Rat's Nest?" Melissa asked.

The giant looked at her.

They both came to a stop.

The giant admired the boat; Melissa could feel a sting of panic beginning to rise in her throat.

"Nice isn't it." The giant replied, more of a statement than as a question.

The launch was huge; it was docked at the end of the pier because of its length. On top there was an array of antenna and dishes. The giant pushed the small deck door open then shoved Melissa aboard.

He pushed her down into a cabin and stood in the doorway looking at her.

"We will be a couple of hours. Make yourself comfortable." He told her.

Melissa held her hands up to him. The giant laughed.

"I'm sure you will make do." He told her.

At that he turned and slammed the door behind him, locking it.

Melissa stood still feeling the gentle swell rock the boat. After five minutes two V8 engines rumbled to life shaking the boat until they settled down to a smooth idle.

Melissa stepped to the door and grasped it with both hands trying to twist the handle.

It stayed fast.

She looked down at her hands in frustration.

Clasping her hands together, she pointed her elbows away from each other then tried to yank her wrists apart. Her muscles strained, she could feel her skin beginning to stretch and burn.

The engine noise began to rise and slowly the boat began to move. Melissa looked around the cabin.

There were drawers below a kitchen sink.

She began ripping them open to look for something to use to cut the tape off or use as a weapon.

The drawers were all empty except for a potato peeler.

She sat down in a seat looking at the peeler. It was rusty and old, but that didn't matter. It still had the plastic point at one end.

Melissa managed to slip one wrist around in the tape. She grasped the peeler in as much of a power grip as she could manage and drove the tip through the tape.

She could feel tendons and muscles strain as the tip slowly slipped through the plastic. After twenty minutes the engine noise began to increase until it was loud enough to drown out her rising panic. Ten minutes after that, sweat was beading down her hairline as she struggled to drive the peeler through the last half of the tape.

The assassin climbed from the car then walked to the edge of the pier. The boat was shrinking into the distance, slowly disappearing behind the mountain guarding the port from the open sea.

"Do we know where it's going?" The assassin asked.

The figure in dark clothes turned to him looking him square in the eyes. The ugly scar running through his eye and down his cheek stood out in the afternoon sunlight.

"No, but we are going to find out." He told the assassin.

They both turned and left the marina.

The assassin followed the other figure at a distance. He knew where the club was and hung back.

By the time the two had reached and agreed on a plan it was late afternoon with darkness only a few hours away.

It was the weekend; people were beginning to fill the club. The figure in dark clothes sat low in his car watching the club door.

It still looked the same, same thumping bass, same throng of people who had no idea about the danger that was hidden behind the four walls. The figure stayed watching the entrance for an hour before he began to get restless. Slowly he looked behind him and saw the assassin move into the shadows.

He pushed the door open then climbed out onto the side walk.

An easterly sea breeze was blowing through The Strand bringing with it cold night-time air. The figure strolled along the sidewalk keeping his head down as if deep in thought. He walked past club entrances with thumping noise spilling from the windows and doors being guarded by oversized steroid pumped monsters.

The figure ignored them all.

He glanced across the street; there were two heavy set guys standing at the door looking in opposite directions. The figure stepped off the sidewalk then crossed the street heading straight for the main door. He had his hands in his pockets, eyes fixed dead ahead of him. He pushed past the cue of people to the front starting up the steps until a giant hand stopped him dead.

The figure looked up at the man in front of him.

"Get out of my way." The figure told him quietly.

The doorman smiled and moved to give the figure a hard shove. His shoulder came back then pushed forward.

The man in black read what was about to happen, he quickly stepped to the side, now he was standing to the man's right. The doorman looked across at him, realisation spreading across his face.

The figure stepped towards the doorman quickly as if to step past and disappear into the club. He bumped into him causing the doorman to yelp, dropping him to the ground.

He looked across at the second doorman shaking his head.

Slowly he stepped inside.

He pushed through another set of doors and entered the club.

The music assaulted him from the darkness. He took his hands from his pockets leaving the tazer behind and began to shoulder his way through the pulsing crowd. He headed straight for the door at the back, shoving it open. It was dark in the long hallway. He stepped in and closed the door behind him.

The figure moved rapidly down the length of the hall, he knew time was against him. He broke into a run and hit the outer door of Rossi's office with his shoulder. The door was something you would typically find in a semi secure office, protecting private information or banking documents.

The lock was designed to stop opportunist thieves from getting in.

It didn't stop the figure in black.

The door jamb gave way ripping from the wall with an explosive bang. He stopped in the centre of the room and looked at the next door. He knew this would take more to get through. The figure looked down at the lock on the door and felt frustration build then turn to anger.

He reached inside his jacket to retrieve a small box. He opened it then removed a small amount of plastic explosive. Carefully, he pressed it into the lock then inserted a small detonator. The figure ran a thin wire to a battery then placed it on the floor next to the box. He connected another wire to the battery then pushed a small thin rod in the explosive next to the detonator.

He pressed a button then stepped out into the hallway again. The small box beeped three times then dumped the current from the battery into the detonator.

The lock exploded, the door swung in violently slamming against the wall.

He quickly stepped into the office and began looking for anything that would lead him to Rossi.

He rounded the desk and grasped the first drawer he saw. It was locked.

The figure ground his teeth together, placed the sole of his boot against the desk then ripped the drawer clean from the desk.

Papers and charts scattered all over the floor. The figure bent down to begin leafing through the mess. He picked up a sheaf of paper and read the lines of text.

Slowly, he balled the paper in his fist.

The figure stood and headed for the door. Reaching the end of the hallway he slipped the door open then glanced into the pulsing light and saw the two doormen walking through the crowd followed by two more. He closed the door and walked slowly towards the office again.

Halfway down the hallway he found what he was looking for, a fire alarm button. The man broke the scribed glass with his elbow and hit the button.

Abruptly a siren began to scream causing the thumping bass to stop. The figure ran for the door then pushed it open, it was still dark but people were running for the door. He stepped into the darkness and vanished into the packed crowd.

239

CHAPTER 45

The boat had been moving for an hour. Melissa sat on a small padded seat bolted to the hull of the boat as she struggled to push the tip of the potato peeler through the last of the tape. The tape split with a light snap as the door swung open. She looked up to see a small figure silhouetted against the darkening background. He looked down at her hands.

"You were supposed to sit quietly until we reached the island." The man told her.

He stepped inside the cabin then slammed the door shut.

With the flick of a switch, the room was bathed in soft light.

"You should sit quietly and wait." The man whispered.

He had a look in his eyes that spelt trouble for Melissa.

She had seen that look before.

Rossi stood in the cavern watching people move back and forth. He had people working and sleeping in shifts. But his three chemists were working around the clock to meet the deadline. Barrels of used solvents and chemicals lay stacked in the corners of the cavern.

Rossi watched the trio carefully. They were dead on their feet. The girl staggered from table to table, her mind close to shutting down from the toxins in the air and lack of sleep. Rossi looked across the cavern at the two boys. The larger of the two, Ralph, was carefully measuring out a beaker of acid. His actions were lethargic.

Beside him was the other, he was almost as useless as the girl. But they were still working and producing.

Rossi had calculated if they could make the next six hours then they would be able to fulfill the shipment.

He walked to the far end of the cavern to survey the five caskets. They would only need three to fill.

The remaining two were to ensure there would be no evidence left behind.

He turned and surveyed the cavern once again then checked his watch. He knew the giant's boat was due in soon and he wanted to be there to greet their new guest.

Rossi started for the door and didn't look back.

The man rushed at her. She was still sitting which presented the first of many problems. She knew she wouldn't be able to get to her feet in time.

Another problem was that her wrists were still wrapped in tape, even though she had managed to break it.

It took her precious seconds to free her wrists. Before she could lift her arms the man crashed into her. He used his shoulders to pin her to seat. Melissa pushed her arms back trying to get her hands between them but couldn't find the leverage. She tried to stab him with the potato peeler but the man was too fast, he grabbed her wrist and shook it from her fingers then locked it against the wall above her head. She gasped at the strength in his grip biting against her skin turned raw from the tape.

The man pushed harder against her.

She felt a hard lump rub against her thigh, a hoarse moan escaping his throat.

Her eyes jammed open in disgust.

She began to scream but the man clamped a hand across her lips stifling it in her throat.

"Shut your mouth. We don't want to attract any attention." He whispered.

He abruptly took his hand away to slap her hard across the face.

The man moved quickly, he grabbed a handful of her hair bunching it in his fist then wrenched her from the seat and threw her to the floor. She landed with a thump face down, the air knocked from her lungs.

He was on top of her before she could do anything. She could feel his hands on her butt, kneading her incessantly.

She struggled to push herself up but the man only slammed her to the floor again. It was then she heard the sound of a steel zip being released.

Melissa shivered at the sound.

She kicked out with her right leg receiving a punch to the spine for her effort. The jolt of pain caused her to gasp. Her legs turned numb and wouldn't move, her arms felt as if they were weighted down with lead.

The man's hands began clawing at her once again. Melissa felt fingers slip beneath her, tugging at her belt buckle. She managed to lift an arm but that was it.

Melissa felt her jeans go slack around her waist.

The weight of them on the floor stopped the tough fabric from retreating down her thighs. The man grunted in frustration as he pushed himself up to straddle her.

He grabbed her belt and wrenched her jeans down her legs as far as he could.

Melissa felt a cold rush across her skin as renewed panic took hold.

She pushed her arms under herself then lifted herself from the floor.

The man placed a hand between her shoulder blades shoving her down again.

Melissa crashed down with a gasp. She screwed her eyes shut at the pain that now seemed to be radiating from everywhere.

The man ground his hips against her; Melissa could feel him digging into her. She tried to drag herself forward but the man kept her immobile.

He leaned forward pinning her down.

Melissa turned her head to the right so she couldn't feel his acrid breath on her neck and saw her salvation.

As the man thrust his hips, she screamed, her muscles twitching in pain.

He thrust harder.

Melissa blocked the disgusting feeling from her mind, she stretched out her right arm.

The man ran his tongue along the nape of her neck biting down, drawing blood.

The pain almost paralysed her.

She pushed out further until her fingertips brushed the peeler. Melissa gathered it in her fingers clenching it tight.

She felt a blinding rage build inside her and began to scream as loud as she could.

The man stopped moving for a fraction of a second.

Melissa took advantage.

She arced the potato peeler behind her as hard as she could muster stabbing at the man's head directly behind her own. Her frenzied attack caught the man by surprise, the first blow stabbing him directly in his right eye.

He howled in pain and fell sideways landing on the floor. Melissa rolled away and sprung to her feet. She quickly yanked her jeans around her waist fastening the buttons.

The man was on his hands and knees, blood streaming from the gaping hole in his head. She took two quick steps towards him, her right foot connecting with his chin. The man dropped to the floor in an inert heap on his back.

Melissa looked down at him as he moaned. She bent down taking him in her hand and squeezed hard.

The sting she felt made her rage boil.

She lifted the potato peeler high above her.

"Go ahead, finish the job." A voice called from behind her.

The giant stood in the doorway, he had seen what had happened and was repulsed by it.

Melissa turned to look. The giant just stood there, waiting.

"I said finish what was started." The giant told her in a louder voice.

She turned back to the man on the floor.

His eyes snapped open at the sound of the giant's voice.

He looked to the doorway then at Melissa.

He started to say something but didn't get the words out.

Melissa drove the peeler deep into the tip of his penis.

Chapter 46

The giant stepped into the cabin and grasped the man around the neck.

His fingers dug in then began to squeeze.

Slowly, carefully, the giant lifted him from the floor of the boat. The man clawed at the giant as he held him at arms length.

"You shouldn't have touched her like that." The giant told him in a dead voice.

"You know that isn't the way we do things." The giant carried on.

The man gagged, his face turning blue. He desperately tried to break the giant's grip but to no avail. The man's jeans fell to the floor. The giant looked down, the peeler buried deep in the softening flesh.

The giant turned to Melissa.

"Excuse me." He said quietly.

The giant stepped for the door, the man still in his outstretched grip. He walked through the door then slammed it shut.

Melissa stood still listening to the drone of the engines, her legs turned to jelly and she collapsed to the floor. A sob heaved her chest as two gunshots echoed through the boat.

After a moment the giant cracked the door open then stepped into the cabin. He looked down at Melissa, his face devoid of emotion. Slowly he bent down, squatting in front of her.

His eyes betrayed nothing; just an empty stare studied her.

Melissa wiped at the tears on her cheeks.

The giant held his hand out.

"You shouldn't have to put up with that." He whispered.

He grabbed her hand, lifting her to her feet.

"He won't bother you again."

The giant pointed to another door in the cabin.

"There is a bathroom through that door." The giant stated.

He turned and left the room without saying another word.

It was full dark by the time the boat manoeuvred between the rocks into the small bay of the island. The Captain gently beached the boat on the sand while the giant readied the heavy plank for everyone to disembark.

The boat slid to a stop as the Captain gunned the engines to wedge the hull firmly in the sand.

The giant slid the plank over the side.

Lights shone from the cabins buried in the sparse bush casting shadows against the white hull of the boat lighting up the small cove.

Rossi was standing on the white sand waiting for them. The giant walked to the rear of the boat and opened the cabin door. Melissa sat in one corner as far from the door as she could get. Her hands balled into fists and jammed under her arms.

"Time to go." The giant told her.

Melissa glanced sideways at him.

"I think I'll stay here." She whispered.

The giant sighed.

"No, you won't." He said as he stepped into the room.

Melissa watched him move towards her and pressed herself against the wall involuntarily.

She knew it was irrational, if he had wanted to hurt her he had plenty of chances before now, she told herself.

"Get off the boat." The giant told her.

There was no anger in his voice.

Melissa stayed where she was.

If he wanted her off the boat then he was going to have to forcibly remove her from it.

The giant sighed and shrugged his shoulders.

"Have it your way then."

He moved quickly across the room to grab her by the arm. The strength of his grip startled her but she forced herself to stay focused.

As the giant lifted her from the floor, Melissa sprang to her feet. Her hand came away from her side; she lifted it high in the air exposing a broken shard of glass.

Melissa eyed the thick muscle at the side of the giant's neck, bringing it down hard and fast but the giant spun out of the way at the last moment.

The shard of glass glanced off his collar bone and drove deep into the thick muscle on his chest.

The giant howled, more in anger than pain.

He released his grip on her arm swatting her away as if she were nothing more than an insect.

Melissa tumbled to a stop against the door of the cabin. She looked up at the giant, the flash of anger gone. It had been replaced by his calm dead exterior once again.

He looked down at the piece of glass embedded deep in his chest then slowly cast his gaze at Melissa.

"That was a bad idea." He told her in an icy voice.

Carefully, he gripped the piece of glass between two fingers and slipped it from the wound.

Melissa began to shake. He showed nothing, no pain, no emotion of any kind.

The glass clinked to the ground shattering into a thousand tiny bloody pieces.

"Last chance, get off the boat." He told her.

Melissa quickly rose to her feet.

"No." She told him flatly.

The giant turned and rushed towards her. He was on top of her before she could say or do anything. He picked her up then pushed her through the doorway stepping quickly up to the railing and stopped.

"Don't say I didn't warn you."

He lifted her over the side then dropped her overboard.

Chapter 47

Dan reached the port as the sun was beginning to set on the horizon. He worked his way through town and reached the bridge linking Tauranga with Mount Maunganui then skidded to a halt.

To his left was the marina, to the right, would take him to the industrial port. He turned left heading for the marina, it was closer.

Dan pulled to a stop and climbed out of the car. He looked around but couldn't see anyone, anywhere. He flipped his phone open to scroll through the call log until he found the number then pressed send. The phone went straight through to a mailbox.

He swore as the phone told him what to do then left a message.

His phone chirped.

Dan looked at it then answered the call.

"Yes."

"Be at the airport in twenty minutes." The accented voice told him.

"Where's Emery?" Dan shouted at the phone.

"Busy. Airport. Twenty minutes."

"How will I find you?" Dan asked.

The connection severed. He looked at his phone and swore again.

Dan glanced at his watch. It was twenty to seven in the evening.

Dan climbed back into the car then pulled out of the parking lot driving slowly down the road to cross the harbour bridge and towards the airport.

He pulled onto a side road then drove through an open gate that would take him to a row of new hangers that had been built opposite the terminal.

Lights bathed the road edge of the hangers in a soft yellow light.

Dan pulled off the end of the road turning the car around so he could see the entire length of asphalt and whoever drove in or out. His watch told him he was ten minutes ahead of time.

So he settled in to wait.

The assassin watched the figure climb into his car and take off toward the harbour bridge. He gathered his phone from the passenger seat and dialled a number. It was answered after the third ring.

"Dan has been rerouted to the airport, I assume that is where we are heading?" The assassin asked.

"Yes." The line severed.

The assassin tailed Dan over the bridge covering the distance to the airport in less than ten minutes.

As they reached the airport the assassin had a sinking feeling in the pit of his stomach that the situation was about to spiral out of control.

The assassin entered the ring road following it as it snaked around to an unmarked hanger. As the car turned a corner at the end of the road, the assassin saw an unmarked police car parked on the grass with a person sitting in the front seat.

He continued around the corner then parked on the grass in front of an open hanger.

The assassin climbed out and stood in front of the dark gaping hole.

"I've got a feeling this is about to get a whole lot worse." The assassin mumbled.

Dan rounded the corner of the hanger to see someone standing on the edge of the darkness. Slowly he walked towards him. When Dan was six feet away, he heard a soft hum and the hanger next to him exploded in soft light.

The assassin turned and looked at him.

"I see you made it." He stated.

"Where is Emery?" Dan asked.

The assassin just pointed into the hanger.

Behind a sleek black Aerospatiale AS 350 helicopter, a figure was busy stuffing hardware into a black bag.

Together they walked towards the rear of the hanger.

"Where the hell have you been?" Dan asked.

"Dead." I told him.

I touched the fresh scar running down my cheek. The vision in my left eye was still blurry but the doctor told me it would heal in time.

I turned to face him.

The butterfly stitches holding the skin together itched. The doctor told me I was lucky the shard of glass hadn't run deeper than it did.

"What the hell happened to your face?" He asked.

"The explosion went off a little too early." I told him.

Dan looked at the assassin.

"That's Calum, don't ask how we met." I told him.

Dan shook his head in confusion.

"What the hell is going on. Why did you disappear?" He asked.

"Rossi had Amy kidnapped." I told him.

"The same Rossi we were after for the drugs?" Dan asked.

I just nodded and passed a bag loaded with gear to Calum. I grabbed the handles of another two bags then loaded them into the rear of the helicopter.

"You killed Martin, didn't you?" Dan asked.

I could hear something hostile in his voice and looked across at Calum.

I nodded.

"He had it coming."

"Huh, I suppose he did. Still…"

The punch caught me square on my already cut cheek. My head snapped to the side, the stitches tore open, blood flowed down my cheek.

Before he could land another Calum was standing in front of him, a silenced pistol at his forehead.

I touched my cheek then slowly turned to look at Dan.

"That really wasn't necessary." I told him calmly.

I could see fury in Dan's eyes.

He said nothing.

"Save that for Rossi. He's the one who has Amy, that's where we're going." I told him.

Dan nodded reluctantly.

Calum slowly lowered the pistol then tucked it in a hidden holster.

"We don't need this gentlemen, sort this out when we get back, ok?" Calum stated.

"Emery, they kidnapped someone else." Dan told me.

I glanced at him.

"Who?" I asked.

"A cop. She's from Auckland. Name's Melissa."

I looked at Calum.

"She's DEA, on loan from Miami. She got sold out by someone, that part we needed Martin to figure out." I told him.

Dan looked more annoyed that we hadn't included him in our disappearing act, but I still needed someone to be looking for Amy. He would have found her eventually but we were fast running out of time.

Dan stayed quiet for a moment. I could see him thinking hard about the situation.

"Why did you fake your death?" He asked.

"I wanted Rossi to panic and make a mistake." I answered simply.

A door slammed behind us and a tall blond man walked towards us. He was carrying a helmet and dressed in a flight suit to combat the cold. He walked past us then placed his gear on the pilots seat.

The machine sat on a dedicated trolley built with heavy duty rubber tyres and an aluminium platform.

He grabbed the handle then heaved the AS350 out of the hanger into the darkness. He walked back inside past us to a switch board.

"Ok, lights off." The pilot told us.

The hanger turned dark. I could see the silhouettes of Dan and Calum against the city background. The pilot walked up to us and gazed at us in turn.

I turned to him.

"We all ready Mack?" I asked.

He nodded in the darkness then turned and walked for the pilot's door.

Calum and I turned to walk for the helicopter leaving Dan standing in the darkness.

I realised he wasn't with us, I turned and looked back into the darkness.

"You coming with us or staying here?" I asked.

"What are you going to do out there Emery?" He asked in return.

"I don't know yet but there is a boat due in soon and we are going to stop that shipment from leaving the island." I told him.

I turned and continued towards the helicopter.

As I climbed aboard, Mack touched the starter. The igniters cracked violently as the turbine spooled up and began to scream. Soon the rotors were a blur against the shimmering lights of Tauranga city's skyline. I pulled a headset on then thumbed the microphone button.

"All set here Mack." I told him.

I went to close the door but a hand stopped me.

"Hold one." I told Mack.

Dan climbed in and looked across the cabin at me.

"Ok. Let's get moving."

Mack pushed the throttle forward then gently raised the collective pulling the torque meter into the green zone.

The AS350 lifted effortlessly into the night sky turning north east towards the island.

Chapter 48

The boat's lights blinked brightly on the horizon. It was right on schedule according to the timetable the Captain had been given. They had two hours to meet the deadline, the boat still had at least an hour to travel before it would reach the rendezvous point to pick up the shipment.

The giant turned on the small pier then walked down the brightly lit tunnel towards the cavern. The three chemists were still preparing the drugs even as the ship neared. Rossi was panicking.

The giant shoved his hands into his pockets and kept walking. He was thinking about what he would do after this had ended. He wondered if he would stay in New Zealand assisting Rossi or if he would take his cut of the profits then vanish.

He had heard the fishing was good up around the Alaskan coast.

The walk back to the cavern took him twenty minutes at a fast pace. He stepped into the cavern looking at the chaos of activity taking place around him then slapped a set of switches, the tunnel filled with darkness and the heavy cavern door began to close.

Three of the five coffins were almost filled to the brim. The remaining two were empty, staying that way until the very end.

The giant crossed the cavern passing Amy.

Her eyes were wide, her mind, operating on adrenaline alone.

The giant shook his head feeling a twinge of remorse.

Rossi checked his watch as the giant approached.

"The drop is at one. In another fifteen minutes get the caskets ready for transport to the coast." Rossi called over the rising noise.

The giant just nodded then walked to the scales on which the caskets sat. He gazed at the weight on the digital readout while leaning against the rock wall to wait for the remaining keys to be packaged then placed in the casket.

A man came over carrying a large tray and a Russian AK47. He upended the tray with four wrapped bundles of drugs into the last coffin tipping the scales past the contracted amount. The giant pushed himself off the rock wall indicating to the man to grab the other end of the casket lid. They heaved it up to place it gently on the wooden box. The giant hefted a nail gun in his right hand then started sealing the lid shut.

The pneumatic thump echoed around the cavern.

Amy jerked her head up and looked towards the giant.

Dirk stopped what he was doing, turning his attention to the noise.

He dropped the beaker he was holding and slowly slumped against the wall behind him. They had been working for weeks on end and he was exhausted.

Amy sunk to her knees, she was soon asleep on the stone floor.

Melissa was perched on a chair in the corner of the room. She was locked in a cabin with no windows. She had tried the door once, put her shoulder against the surface then pushed hard.

It didn't move.

Sitting back down, she asked herself why she was here, she was having a hard time putting everything together. She knew the drugs were coming from the island; that part was obvious to her. What she didn't understand was how Amy was tied up with it all. She had been sitting for what felt like hours when the door swung open, a small man stepped in pointing a pistol at her. In his other hand he held a pair of hand cuffs. He was barely five foot four, Melissa towered over him.

"Rossi wants to give you the grand tour. Stand up." He told her.

Melissa stood, but she didn't move. Her eyes locked onto the small man's and stayed there watching his reactions. On the outside she was calm, hiding the fact that underneath her heart was thumping in her chest.

"Turn and face the wall." The man told her.

Melissa kept her hands by her side then turned to face the wall. The man stepped slowly behind her.

He slipped the pistol into his holster then snapped a leather strap over the grip to keep it in place. The man stepped directly behind her then grabbed a wrist to snap a cuff around it.

Her foot shot up, the heel of her boot catching the man in the groin. He bent forward at the waist gasping as he slowly dropped to his knees. Melissa turned quickly and drove the knuckles of her right hand down onto the back of his neck.

Delicate bone and vital links from the brain to the body.

His head snapped forward and the man collapsed to the floor.

She shook her hand, trying to rid the throbbing in her knuckles, then grabbed the pistol from the holster and snatched the man's radio.

Carefully she poked her head around the doorframe looking into the darkness. Dull lights were glowing between the trees casting slow moving shadows on the cabins. Melissa looked out across the bay but could only see darkness. The sound of the ocean gently breaking against the sandy shore.

Voices floated out of the cabins.

Slowly, quietly, she stepped into the darkness and made her way towards the main cabin area.

Melissa slipped the pistol into the waistband of her jeans as she silently stepped through the sparse forest.

She stopped abruptly, listening as a door opened and three men stepped out. They carried flash lights, the beams dancing around the trees. Melissa chanced a quick look in an eye level window and saw a mirror covered in white powder. Bottles of liquor sat half empty on the table, a man passed out on the floor. She turned then stepped quietly into the forest and up a small rise where she could see over the roofs of the low lying cabins.

Her first thought was to get to the boat. If she could get to the boat then she stood a chance of escaping. But two things stopped her. First she had to find Amy, get her away from here, second, she knew nothing about boats.

Frustration was beginning to turn to anger when she saw flash lights moving in the scrub. A hundred metres away the three men were walking into the bush. She sunk low to the ground watching them disappear.

The boat was unguarded. She thought about sinking it but quickly realised time was against her.

Instead she did what she had to.

Melissa turned and ran into the bush to follow the men. It didn't take her long to locate them.

She hung back, moving from tree to tree to keep herself hidden.

The darkness closed in around the trees as they moved deeper into the bush, she estimated that they had been moving for close to an hour when they stopped.

Melissa peered into the darkness, the flashlights trained on a small cabin.

The door swung open and a man stepped out.

He was carrying something in his hands. She guessed it was some kind of weapon.

Melissa was too far away to hear what was being said between them. She crouched behind a tree holding her breath trying to catch something, anything that would help her find Amy.

She watched them intently as they moved into the small hut. The door slammed shut and slowly the flashlights all disappeared. Melissa waited twenty minutes in silence. In the distance she could hear the ocean breaking against rocks on the island coastline, above that she thought she heard a faint humming sound but it was lost to the background noise.

Melissa moved out of the darkness edging closer to the small shack. She wanted to see inside, maybe Amy was in there.

A window faced towards her; quietly she made her way through the undergrowth until she was three feet from the wall. With the pistol in her hand she inched closer to the window to peer inside.

It was empty.

She slowly stood up then quietly moved to the door to gently push it open. Inside the shack took on a whole different feeling.

It was strongly built and secure. At her feet was another heavy door, it was open, leading down into darkness.

Melissa closed the door to the shack behind her, silently checked the pistol was loaded then stepped into the darkness.

CHAPTER 49

Mack pulled the AS350 into a shallow turn around the northern side of the island to follow the coast. We were at fifteen hundred feet and moving at eighty knots. I leaned out into the breeze to scan the coastline through night vision goggles. The landscape turned bright green showing flaring ship lights on the horizon winking at me. Ocean liners arriving and leaving the port moved silently past and out to sea, or slipped in behind Mount Maunganui.

"Emery, what's that?" Mack asked through the headset.

I lifted the goggles to see him pointing down at a small beacon light nestled in a tight cove.

I slipped the goggles back in front of my eyes and gazed at the area below us.

The coastline was rugged. Jagged rocks worn smooth by the sea pointed at the sky towards us. I could barely make out the light, it was so dull. The landscape followed a definite line against the ocean telling me that the rock face was sheer, the ocean around it deep.

The heat signature was slight but definite.

"Can we get down there?" I asked.

Mack dropped the collective putting the helicopter into a slow descent. The airspeed bled off as the dim light grew slowly brighter and larger.

The helicopter levelled out, the altimeter showed we were a hundred feet above sea level. I gazed at the small beacon light. It was fixed to the end of a small jetty, beyond that there was a tunnel disappearing into the cliff face.

I could see a small set of railway tracks disappearing into the green void of the tunnel. I lifted the goggles as I turned to Calum and Dan.

"There is a tunnel that goes into the cliff face." I pointed behind me then thumbed the mike.

"Mack, can you get us any closer?" There was silence for a moment. Then he shook his head.

"No. I can get closer, directly over the jetty but the drop will be a hundred feet at least. Otherwise we will be chopping rock."

I looked out the door at the small light and wiped at a small trickle of blood on my cheek. I sat there thinking how we were going to get to the small jetty, then the microphone clicked.

"How about a ride on the long line?" Mack asked.

I looked over the seat at him. There was a smirk on his lips.

"Ok, just don't button me at the wrong time. That water looks cold." I told him.

"Ok, I saw a small clearing at the top of the cliff. We'll land and get set up."

Mack raised the collective and the AS350 climbed into the night sky. He leaned out the right hand door lining the skids for the dead centre of the small clearing, the rotor disk barely clearing the trees.

I climbed out followed by Calum and Dan. I reached inside to grab the handle of a large nylon bag then dragged it across the floor towards the door. I opened the zip grabbing a coiled nylon rope and began to unravel it. One end was spliced into a loop with a tough aluminium eyelet. I crawled under the helicopter and attached it to the hook.

Calum and Dan had picked a harness each out of the bag and were climbing into them. I collected the remaining end then attached the climbing karabiner to the front of Calum's harness. We collected the small bags from the helicopter and slung weapons over our shoulders.

"I'll send Dan after you." I called to him over the noise of the turbine.

Calum nodded giving the thumbs up.

I nodded and walked to the pilot's door giving Mack the signal to spool up and lift off.

The engine began to whine and the helicopter lifted effortlessly into night sky. One hundred feet later, Calum disappeared into the darkness. I slipped the night vision goggles over my eyes to watch from the cliff top. The scene was a dull fluorescent green. Mack dropped height and swung Calum out over the water. He lined the end of the jetty up then began to swing Calum on the end of the rope like a pendulum. On the third swing Mack lowered the collective at the same time Calum was over the edge of the jetty.

Calum touched down effortlessly quickly releasing the karabiner from his harness. Thirty seconds later, Dan was disappearing into the darkness.

Mack returned and I clipped onto the long line. Suddenly the line snapped taut and I lifted into the darkness, the helicopter thundering above me.

Mack repeated the procedure a third time, hovering, waiting for the line to release. He thumbed the radio.

"There is a small island five minutes out. I'll be there within radio if needed."

I gave the thumbs up and the AS350 disappeared into the darkness.

The noise receded to nothing leaving only the sound of an angry ocean pounding the rocks with relentless energy. I motioned to Dan and Calum to follow.

The night vision goggles made progress in the near total darkness much easier but as it was, we still had to tread carefully.

Two rail tracks were raised above the ground supported by sleepers every foot. I looked off into the darkness and wondered how deep the tunnel went into the cliff face. After a hundred metres the tunnel broke out of the cliff side and was suddenly surrounded with a sparse forest. I stopped and looked up at the hill in front of me. I turned and looked at Calum and Dan.

"I'll go over, you two follow the tracks." Calum nodded then disappeared into the darkness.

"How do you know they are down there?" Dan asked.

I turned to him looking at his ghostly figure through the goggles. "I don't."

Carefully, I stepped off the tracks and climbed to the top of the hill. I turned to get my bearings on the tracks then spun one hundred and eighty degrees. As long as the tracks stayed straight I would be OK.

I disappeared into the darkness at pace.

Chapter 50

Melissa placed a foot onto the first concrete step then stopped. Her heart was hammering in her chest. She took a deep breath to calm herself, standing still for what seemed like an eternity. Her weight was on her front foot and her leg was beginning to ache. She took another deep breath then stepped down to the next step.

The door below her opened and voices floated up on a wave of hot acrid air.

Melissa backed out of the stairwell, quickly.

She had to get down the stairs; the fumes rising from below told her she was in the right place.

She silently closed the door then ran a short distance into the bush, away from the small shack.

From her vantage point she could see a small portion of the window along with most of the roof.

Then he appeared.

The giant who had brought her here. Behind him were two more smaller men. Still large but a lot smaller than the giant. Melissa tried to wait patiently but she could feel time ticking away, worry about Amy and whomever else they had down there began to gnaw at her.

The giant stopped outside and turned to the two men with him. She could clearly hear what they were saying now.

"Go and get her, Andrew should have brought her here by now. We have to get her and the other three into the last two coffins in half an hour. The boat is going to be here soon so get moving." The giant told them.

Melissa could clearly hear his high pitched voice tinged with stress.

Melissa figured she had ten minutes to do something before they realised she wasn't where she was suppose to be.

"This is going to be a good payday." One of the guys said, a smile creeping over his face.

The giant nodded in the dull light spilling from the shack.

"Now go, we don't have long." He motioned for the two men to go then swung wildly in Melissa's direction.

I had sped through the undergrowth as quickly as I could, not worrying about concealing noise. I didn't know how far I had to go so wanted to move as quickly as possible. I had moved for what seemed like hours and miles but was in actual fact only a kilometre. I stopped and swung my gaze around searching for anything out of the ordinary amongst the undergrowth but saw nothing.

Slowly I stepped forward.

Straight onto an unseen dry stick.

My heel came down with enough speed that I couldn't stop before it exploded in half.

It sounded like a gun shot.

Silently I cursed myself as I dropped to the forest floor.

A sudden movement to my front and left caught my attention.

The green glow of the surrounding area merged and blurred objects together, but from the distance I could see someone looking towards me.

Someone huge.

The figure pointed towards me then two others ran into the undergrowth momentarily disappearing from sight.

I had to move.

The last thing I needed was to be caught out in the open.

I stepped silently to my left. If they were coming for me then I was going to meet them head on.

I took cover behind a tree. Its base was three feet wide. I looked up to see it disappear into the sky. Its canopy merged with those around it creating a patchy cover.

I dropped to one knee and slid the Beretta from its holster. I didn't bother checking to see if a round was chambered, I had already been through that half a dozen times on the flight out.

I screwed a suppressor to the muzzle feeling the weight shift forward in my hand as I locked it home. It balanced the pistol perfectly for me so I knew exactly where the point of impact would be.

Twigs snapped in the darkness, the green glow of the night vision goggles didn't show me anything other than thin vegetation on the floor of the island.

Slowly I looked from left to right. The Beretta following the arc. I heard movement to my left and carefully turned towards it.

Then it happened.

There was a gunshot. Wood splintered above me. I rolled to my right and zeroed in on the man standing twenty feet away.

The trigger broke and the Beretta coughed twice. A ragged hole formed where the man's nose should have been, he fell to the forest floor behind a small scrubby bush.

Then there was the familiar chatter of submachine gun fire as splashes of dirt kicked up in front of me. I rolled to my right behind a tree pressing my back against it, frantically looking over my shoulders.

I wasn't in a good place.

I heard rustling to my left and right, I figured they were trying to flank me on either side so I had to make a decision, fast.

Quickly I stood, turning to face left. My right arm moved around the trunk of the tree as I carefully pushed around it.

Then there was a scream.

I stopped dead still and listened. I could hear scuffling, small braches and twigs being broken.

"Bring her here!" The giant yelled.

There was another muted scream that was cut off, then silence. I could hear nothing other than a gentle sea breeze moving through the tops of the trees.

"Come out Emery."

I stayed still.

"I won't ask again." The high pitched voice called.

My mind raced through the limited options I had.

"Last chance Emery, come out or she dies." The voice taunted.

I slowly placed my head on the trunk I was leaning against.

All other options had just been taken away.

CHAPTER 51

Calum and Dan moved quickly through the pitch darkness of the tunnel. The tracks pitched and moved over the uneven rock as it sank deeper into the island. Calum glanced at his watch then looked back at Dan. The green environment around them blended into nothingness in front and behind them. Calum turned then stepped forward thumbing the bolt closed on the MP5. It slammed home with a metallic thump, a split second later the same noise echoed behind him. They moved forward quickly, sticking to the jagged walls where they could, offering less of a target for anyone hidden in the tunnel.

Calum stopped abruptly and sniffed the air.

"You smell that?" He asked.

Dan nodded in the darkness. He could smell it. The sharp stench of chemicals underlined with sweat and fear.

They both made to step forward then stopped as a string of overhead lights flicked on flaring the goggles over their eyes.

Calum quickly pulled the goggles from his face and blinked a few times as his eyes adjusted to the harsh light.

Up ahead they could see a giant steel door anchored into the rock around them. The tunnel flared around it allowing it to swing wide open. Calum estimated the door to be twenty feet across and at least ten feet high. Slowly they pressed themselves against opposite walls, muzzles towards the door.

It was then that a dull booming sound echoed towards them down the tunnel. The door moved with light spilling out from behind it.

The giant shoved me down the steps. He had my Beretta in his oversized hand, pressing the muzzle into the area between my shoulders as we walked down the stairs. In front of me the remaining guy had the cop called Melissa pressed close to him.

Her arm was wedged up high behind her back between her shoulder blades with a pistol to the side of her head.

I kept my arms dangling by my sides; I didn't want to give the giant a reason to shoot me, not yet.

We reached the bottom of the stairs. The guy in front let go of Melissa's arm. She slowly dropped it, groaning as it hung limply beside her. The guy swapped the pistol to his other hand then griped the back of her neck shoving her hard into the smooth rock wall next to the door.

He shoved the pistol into a holster then removed a key from his pocket to jam it into a small lock and turned it. The locked snicked open then he shoved the door inwards. Light spilled out of the opening followed by a sharp smell and the chaos of noise.

He closed his hand around Melissa's neck manhandling her into the cavern. The giant shoved me hard in the back. I half turned glancing at him but he saw it coming. The muzzle of my pistol inches from my right eye.

"Don't try anything stupid Emery." He told me over the racket from the doorway.

I held his gaze a second longer then turned to follow Melissa and the man into the cavern.

I looked up, the ceiling of the cavern lifted away, partially disappearing under the powerful lights. The place was huge, blasted from solid rock. Slowly I surveyed the area. Tables rested on trestles holding all sorts of equipment.

Beakers, flasks, Bunsen burners.

The kind of stuff I remembered from my high school days. Only on a much larger scale.

There were two young guys slumped against the slick rock walls, their heads between their knees, eyes closed. I cast my eyes across the room and saw a small figure lying on the floor.

Amy.

"So, Emery. It's good to see you again." A voice called to me.

I looked in the direction of the voice as the giant shoved me in the back again with my pistol.

I was getting sick of that.

I stepped around some tables, Rossi walked across the floor towards us.

I ignored him and kept looking around the room. I counted twelve guys. All shouldering submachine guns and all looking very on edge.

Which made me on edge.

A stray round into a barrel of whatever they were holding here to cut the drugs could explode. And being that the pressure wave would likely set off those around it and being contained underground, anything in the cavern would be instantly turned to vapour.

Rossi stepped in front of me, commanding my attention.

"It's good to see you again." He repeated.

I said nothing.

"As you can see we are ready for our shipment to leave. I must admit, the deadline was being cut very close but we will make the date. Our very dedicated team managed to fulfil the order." He stated as he half turned to sweep the area with an open arm.

I looked across at Amy. She hadn't moved in the five minutes we had been there. The other two had managed to lift their eyes to glance at us then had dropped their heads again.

Rossi shifted his attention to Melissa.

The look on his face made my skin crawl.

"We found her in the woods. It think she was trying to rescue Amy." The giant told Rossi.

Rossi nodded but didn't take his eyes from hers.

"I guess that means Andrew is dead then." He surmised.

There was a tense moment then a guy with a machine gun appeared at Rossi's side.

"Sir the caskets are nailed and sealed shut." He told him.

Rossi nodded.

"Ok, it's time to fill the last two." He said glancing at me with a smile.

The man with the machine gun nodded then stepped away.

Rossi kept his eyes on me, watching for my reaction.

I stayed still.

The guy rounded the tables towards the two young guys sitting on the floor. As he neared them he drew a pistol. From the distance I couldn't tell what kind it was but I didn't need to know, only the reason.

The guy stepped up to the first holding the muzzle inches from his head. I knew what was about to happen and tensed.

The giant sensed it and jammed the muzzle of my pistol into the back of my neck.

"Don't even think about it." He whispered to me.

There were two short blasts and the bodies lay limp on the floor. Scarlet blood already running along the cracks in the stone.

I looked across at Amy. She sat up abruptly, pushing herself against the rock wall, her eyes jammed wide open.

Rossi looked at me.

"They, along with you and your friend here are going to fill the last two caskets." He said with a smirk.

"You aren't going to leave this place alive." I told him.

The smirk left his face. Only disgust and hatred remained.

"You can threaten me as much as you like Emery. I win, you lose." He stated plainly.

Then like a switch it was gone and the smile came back.

He waved and the guy ran back.

"Get them and grab the girl. It's time to close up here." He told him not taking his eyes from me.

Rossi turned then strode away as the guy darted towards the bodies.

The giant shoved me in the back with the pistol again.

That was the last time he was going to do that I had decided.

I followed Rossi between the tables and watched out of the corners of my eyes as armed men grab the three hostages and began dragging them towards the caskets.

Towards the large door at the end of the cavern near the rail tracks.

Towards Calum and Dan.

CHAPTER 52

The door was swinging open from right to left. Calum motioned for Dan to get behind him. Dan skipped across the tracks then pressed himself to the rock wall dropping to one knee. His MP5 trained on the slow moving door, the gap was slowly opening.

"Ok, now what?" Dan asked.

Calum said nothing for a moment.

"At best there are two captives in there. At worst...." The sentence trailed off.

"Just pick your targets and be damned sure they aren't carrying." Calum finished.

Calum fished into his pack and brought out a flash bang grenade. He turned and glanced at Dan.

"We aren't waiting for the door to be wide open." He told him as he ripped the pin from the handle.

Calum turned to aim for the gap that was now four feet wide. He drew his arm back then lobbed the grenade for the gap. Dan watched it sail through the air and bounce off the rock wall.

They both turned away knowing the blinding flash and concussive blast that was about to happen.

We walked slowly towards the rear of the cavern. I could see a large door shut tight against the back wall and five caskets sitting off to my left. We were thirty feet from the door. Melissa was behind me with the giant behind her. As we neared the door a motor began to whine, metal scraping against rock. Slowly the door began to swing outwards, into the tunnel. Rossi stopped to watch the door swing open.

I kept my eyes on the opening and saw it a split second before everyone else.

The small canister bounced off the wall sliding to a stop right at Rossi's feet. He looked down at it in curiosity.

I knew what it was and didn't wait to react.

I turned and dove at Melissa, catching her across the chest knocking her to the floor at the giant's feet. He looked down at us with a confused look which quickly changed to realisation.

The grenade was six feet from us. I hugged Melissa into me and buried one side of my head into my shoulder and screwed my eyes shut.

The blast from the flash bang grenade lit the cavern up like a lightning bolt.

The explosion echoed from the solid rock walls rocketing around the enclosed space like thunder.

Rossi fell over backwards upending a nearby table, spilling the contents on to the stone floor.

Then all hell broke loose.

There was a rifle shot followed closely by the chatter of machine gun fire. The door kept opening slowly.

I glanced up to see Calum burst through the gap followed closely by Dan, their MP5's shouldered, the muzzles crackling with flame.

I sensed the giant behind me dive to his right. He rolled into a ball and hid behind a drum.

He was more agile than I gave him credit for.

Quickly I scrambled to my feet leaving Melissa sprawled on the floor. My ears were ringing. I stepped forward then placed a boot on Rossi's chest and pressed down hard. My fist came back then I felt a sting on my back, then another. The force of the bullets knocked me off balance and I fell forward. Rossi rolled over and began scrabbling away. I looked up, the giant was taking careful aim, straight down the tritium sights, straight at me.

There was a chatter of gunfire followed by another ear shattering explosion. The cavern lit up in bright light. The concussion of the second grenade blew out a section of the overhead lights plunging the end of the cavern into a dull darkness. I moved quickly, not wanting to give the giant a second chance to finish the job.

Calum yanked me to my feet; Dan grabbed Melissa by her hand and pulled her towards the coffins.

"Well, fancy seeing you here." Calum told me over the explosion of AK47 fire.

I looked at him.

"You three get out of here, and close that door. Permanently." I yelled at him.

"Where the hell are you going?" He asked me.

I pointed to the giant as he neared Amy.

"He's got my pistol. I want it back."

Rossi headed for the door leading to the stairwell. There wasn't a lot I could do about it at this point. I crouched behind the coffins and nodded to Dan and Calum.

They both popped up letting an extended burst of fire go, spraying the area.

As I ran I saw three armed men fall to the floor. Bodies littered the bedrock. I jumped over two then cleared a table while the giant grabbed a hold of Amy and lifted her to her feet as if she weighed nothing at all.

I balled my right fist then drove it into the back of the freaks neck. His head snapped forward head butting the stone wall above Amy. The pistol clattered to the floor. I looked at Amy and didn't need to tell her to move.

I took a half step back then powered forward again as the giant half turned. My knee came up catching him high in the kidneys.

He let out a grunt but other than that nothing happened.

"Oh no, you god damn well don't." He snarled.

As he turned, I barely ducked under a round house punch that came at me like a tornado. As I dove, I cocked my right arm and drove it hard into the giant's mid section, just below his sternum.

It wasn't a very good punch, too close. But the effect it had on him was nothing. He didn't even flinch.

I looked up, an evil grin on his face. He brought one hand down on my left shoulder, thumping me to the floor. I felt my collar bone snap like a twig, my left arm went limp. The giant put a heavy boot on my chest then shoved me hard, I could feel my vest grabbing the stone floor as I skidded into an over turned table.

"Big mistake Emery, coming here. You should have just left it well alone." The giant called to me over the rattle of machinegun fire.

As he stepped closer I lifted a leg and snapped a kick into his groin, which only enraged him.

He jumped on me, his crushing weight knocking the air from my lungs. As I turned my head to avoid a head butt I saw the pistol lying just out of reach.

I lifted my good hand and fought for something vulnerable, anything.

My thumb found an eye socket.

I pressed in hard as a punch landed on the side of my cheek tearing open the wound from the explosion. My head began to swim, I could feel blood trickling into my ear. My thumb slipped from his eye leaving just a bloody hole. He looked down at me with his remaining eye and roared in fury.

He drew his fist up lining it squarely with my nose.

I knew this was going to hurt.

The hiss of a suppressor startled me, the giant fell forward smothering me.

I shoved his lifeless body away then looked sideways at the hole in his temple, the size of a ten cent piece.

I turned and saw Amy holding the pistol three feet away, the muzzle moving through small circles as she breathed in and out rapidly.

Carefully I sat up.

Another explosion rocked the cavern.

There were half a dozen guys with guns shooting at a small gap in the door way.

I snatched the gun from Amy then lifted myself to my feet. The room swayed and I toppled sideways into the rock wall.

Amy grabbed me by the hand and draped it over her shoulder. She yanked me forward towards the other end of the cavern, towards the stairwell.

CHAPTER 53

. . . .

As we reached the door, a splash of sparks bounced off the rock walls around us. I spun quickly, three guys had their weapons trained on us from the other end of the cavern. They were a hundred feet away.

I shoved Amy through the door and glanced around quickly.

There was a large pile of rags in one corner of the cavern. Most of them were stained a dirty colour.

I looked across a table, a bunsen burner was on its side, the flame etching the table top a charred black. I stepped forward and picked it up. It was the spirits type of burner. Not the newer type that ran on natural gas.

I stepped back towards the door holding the pistol in my left hand. Every movement sent a jolt of agony through my shoulder then down my arm.

I lined up the pile of rags and threw the burner towards the pile. I had to get it right, too low and the rags could put the flame out.

The glass burner hit the rock a foot above the pile, showering the rags in flammable liquid.

The pile exploded in a bright orange fireball which rapidly accelerated. I stepped through the door as a hail of lead bounced off the rock around me.

The pistol felt heavy in my left hand. Carefully, painfully, I lifted it to take aim at the barrels of ether across the cavern.

I was hoping the fire would set it off, not the projectile.

Gently I squeezed the trigger, the Beretta coughed and a stream of clear liquid began to spray from the side of a barrel.

"Time to go." I yelled at Amy.

I grabbed her by the hand and dragged her stumbling up the steps for the doorway at the top.

Calum threw a grenade at the corner of the door as they retreated down the small tunnel. The blast brought chunks of rock down jamming the door solid.

Dan and Calum ran quickly into the darkness, the echoes of gunfire and yelling behind them, Melissa a step behind.

They kept going until all the noise had stopped, they could only hear the noise of their boots hitting the rock echoing in the tunnel.

They stopped and turned to look back into the darkness.

"You hear that?" Dan asked.

"Aye. It's the ocean. We must be close to the end of the tunnel."

They turned and continued walking.

"How far do we have to go?" Melissa asked.

Before Calum could answer the ground shook, a violent thump. They stopped and turned slowly to look back down the tunnel. Small pinpricks of light began to quickly flair then rapidly grow.

No one said a word; they just turned and ran towards the ocean.

They couldn't tell how far they had to go.

Calum saw the tunnel move out into the hollow. He grabbed Melissa and yanked her sideways. Dan saw it a split second later diving after them. They curled around the edge of the bank as the compressed fireball exploded from the tunnel lighting up the night sky.

We crested the top of the stairs. It took longer than I had thought it would. Everything hurt; blood obscured my left eye and blocked my ear.

I could feel it drying on my skin, shrinking and cracking against movement.

Thankfully the door at the top was open. We climbed out, I grabbed the handle with my good arm and lifted it slowly from the floor then let it slam shut. It felt like the heaviest thing I had ever moved.

Amy thumped the clasp into place then pushed the lock closed. We stumbled out of the cabin into the dark forest.

"We need to move." I told Amy.

As quick as we could, we both followed a well worn path down a gentle slope. We were fifty metres away when there was a muffled thump then the small shack erupted into a fireball. The intense heat singed the hairs on the backs of our necks, the pressure wave threw us off our feet and we crashed to the rocky earth.

I groaned and slowly rolled over. The shack was completely gone. All that remained was a charred black hole in the ground.

Amy helped me to my feet again. She stepped back to look at me in the scattered moonlight.

"Are you ok?" She asked.

I just nodded in the darkness and slowly placed the Beretta back in its holster.

We both turned as we heard the sudden rumble of a boat start up in the distance.

"Rossi." I whispered.

I grabbed Amy's hand and dragged her into the darkness towards the noise of the boat. I knew it was going to be a waste of time but we had to get to the beach before Rossi made it too far out to sea.

I thumbed the radio, all I heard was a static.

I shook my head and cursed.

"How far is it to the beach?" I asked Amy as we ran.

"Maybe a half hour, maybe less." She answered from behind me.

We kept running.

Calum and Melissa crested a ridge onto a clearing in the bush. Dan was already at the top. He had placed red flares around the perimeter and was scanning the dark horizon.

"Mack's on his way in. Should be two minutes."

Melissa lay on her back in the moonlight.

"Are you ok?" Calum asked, his accent cutting through.

She didn't answer, just nodded.

Calum put a hand on her shoulder and felt her tremble. He knew what was coming.

He caught her first sob and was about to say something when the high pitch whine of the AS350 broke through.

Thirty seconds later Mack had settled the helicopter on the make shift pad. Calum opened the door and Melissa climbed into the cabin. Dan climbed in then laced a seat belt around her waist.

"Where's Emery?" Mack asked after Calum had slipped a set of headphones on.

"We lost him. Last I saw he was heading for the opposite door. Don't know if he made it."

Mack shook his head and looked at the red lit instrument panel in front of him.

"Get in. We'll go have a look."

Calum nodded then slid into the passenger seat next to Mack. Five seconds later the helicopter was passing through translation on its way towards the middle of the island.

Mack pulled into a hover then flicked a switch on the collective. The night sun flood light attached to the nose of the aircraft blazed the surrounding area. Its beam was powerful enough to reach the forest floor.

Mack flew in an ever increasing circle, keeping the nose pointing inwards.

"I don't see him." Dan called over the intercom.

"Keep looking." Calum replied.

Mack gave up and started again, this time he gained height in an effort to cover more ground. They could see a wisp of smoke drifting from the hole in the rocky island floor.

He started again, nose in, increasing the circle diameter as he started each new rotation. Mack pulled the nose up into a hover. He flicked another switch then pointed the night sun down on a spot that had caught his attention.

"There. What's that?" Mack asked.

Calum pushed forward in his seat to look towards the centre of the beam.

"Don't know. I can't make it out." Calum looked up, he could see the horizon and the lights from Tauranga city lining it.

Low and to his left, a small light was moving away from the island at speed.

"There." He pointed. Mack looked up.

He pushed the cyclic forward. The nose dipped and soon they were rushing towards the cove at a hundred and twenty knots.

I heard the chopper approaching. It was moving fast. We were stumbling down an incline. I could see a small encampment at the foot of the hill.

As we neared it the chopper broke over us dropping rapidly down into the cove. I skidded to a stop in the sand and watched the blazing light arcing around the water.

It was Mack.

The helicopter pulled into a tight turn and touched down gracefully onto the short beach. Sand and water stung the skin on my face, pushed around by the rotor blast. The rear door slid open at the same time Calum appeared around the nose of the chopper.

He ducked under the rotors and ran towards us.

"I take it that was your handy work back there?" Calum asked.

I just nodded and touched the open scar on my face. Calum's eyes flicked to Amy.

"Amy this is Calum, Calum, Amy." I said by way of introduction.

Amy looked up, her eyes wary.

Calum turned to me.

"We have to move. We saw a boat take off about five minutes ago."

"It's Rossi." I told him confirming his suspicions.

Calum turned and we hurried towards the waiting chopper, Amy trailing behind us.

"Did I tell you, you look like shit?" Calum asked.

I smiled as I answered.

"No, I think you forgot to mention that."

Calum climbed back into the front seat next to Mack. I helped Amy into the rear and pulled the door closed after me. I slipped a headset on slowly trying not to use my left arm.

"Good to have you back." Mack called over the intercom.

I just nodded. After a short silence I keyed the intercom.

"Rossi escaped. You saw a boat heading off shore?" I asked.

"Due south, back towards the Bay." Mack replied.

"I don't want him reaching the shore." I told Mack.

"Roger that."

He pushed the throttle home and lifted the collective off the floor. The AS350 screamed and shot into the night sky.

Mack pushed the left pedal and the helicopter spun violently. In a matter of seconds we were nudging VNE.

CHAPTER 54

J ohn Rossi slammed the drive into reverse then gunned the twin V8's to redline. The engines screamed in protest as the boat shot backwards away from the beach. Without throttling back he jammed the drive in the opposite direction then spun the wheel of the boat for the narrow entrance to the cove.

He hadn't allowed panic to set in, but he could feel it begin to gnaw at him. He knew he had to disappear.

The cartel would be after his blood and they wouldn't stop until they had it.

He knew, somewhere, sometime they would eventually find him and he knew he would be dead. Not just dead, but hacked up into little pieces, slowly and painfully.

The thought made him shudder.

He looked behind him, back towards the island. A thin laser of light appeared over the outer cliff face of the cove facing the ocean. It dipped towards the horizon and began heading straight for him.

Rossi pushed the throttles hard against the stops. The boat lurched and rolled violently in the swell as it rocketed forward towards the coastline. He was pushing along at forty knots, as fast as the boat would go.

But no where near enough to outrun a helicopter.

He reached down to pull a pistol from the map pouch next to the throttles. He slid the magazine out to check it was loaded. The magazine went back into the well. He gripped the slide and pulled it back letting it slam home again then slipped it into his pocket.

Slowly, he brought the throttles back to a cruise turning the boat in a lazy circle.

"Shouldn't take long. I can see his navigation lights from here." Mack called back.

I said nothing. I was busy running through options.

"He's turning." I looked up and saw the navigation lights turn left in a slow wide circle.

"What's the plan?" Mack asked.

I looked down at the boat then the distance to shore. I didn't want him to reach the shore at all, the boat included.

"We have to stop him here, nothing reaches the shore." I told him over the intercom.

I knew Dan and Calum were listening as well.

"I'm getting on that boat." I continued.

Calum turned back to look at me.

"You know that's a really stupid idea, don't you?" He asked.

I said nothing, just pulled the Beretta from its holster then dropped the magazine from the well.

I pulled a fresh one from a pocket on my vest and slipped it into place feeling it click home. Carefully I pulled the slide halfway back and saw a fresh cartridge chambered.

The Beretta slipped back into its holster and I snapped a clasp over the back of the hammer.

Mack thumbed the intercom.

"I'd just like to point out that this is not a good idea. The swell is a couple of metres plus there is a surface wind. If it goes wrong, we are all going down." He told me.

I suddenly noticed the helicopter being buffeted by winds.

I looked back at Calum then pressed the button to talk to Mack.

"Long line it is then." I declared as I started pulling on a harness.

Mack chuckled over the intercom then looked back at me.

"You're a suicide junkie, you know that."

I just grinned as I looped a rope through the karabiner and coiled it at the door ready to be kicked out.

Dan locked one end to a secure eyelet at the centre of the cabin then gave the thumbs up sign.

I pulled myself to my feet and stepped carefully towards the door.

"As soon as that rope goes out you go after it, can't risk getting it caught in the tail rotor." Mack called to me.

I nodded then pulled the door open and placed a foot onto the skid.

Mack pulled the AS350 into a tight turn to chase the boat.

I watched out the side as the boat straightened then took off again. This time heading out towards the horizon and millions of square miles of water.

Mack flared briefly to match the speed of the boat and gazed down through the Lexan floor window. He could see Rossi looking back up at him, a grimace on his face.

Mack lowered the collective bringing the helicopter to fifty feet of the boat. He was directly above it travelling at forty knots.

I looked down, Rossi was looking back at me.

It was now or never.

With my right foot I kicked the rope out, a split second later I jumped after the coil as the wind caught it to haul it rearward.

I covered the fifty feet in a near freefall. I could feel the rope tear through my gloved hand and grabbed it just in time. I thumped down landing on one knee. I snapped a knife out slicing through the rope in one movement.

My arm throbbed and my head thumped.

Rossi watched in disbelief as he saw me jump from a moving helicopter onto the boat. It was then he snatched the gun from a hidden pocket and levelled it at me. I stopped moving, the rope free and swinging away. Rossi throttled the boat back bringing the engines to idle.

"Wrong time, wrong place, Mister Blackstone." Rossi said to me.

I said nothing.

I could hear Mack hovering in the background as the boat bobbed and danced in the swell. I knew Calum and Dan would have crosshairs on the boat but I guessed the movement would be hard to keep it accurate.

Rossi stepped forward; he was three feet from me. I still held the knife in my hand but he was out of reach.

The spotlight played over the boat shining directly on Rossi. He squinted raising his free hand to block the light.

I could feel a warm sticky ooze on my left cheek. It ran down my neck into the vest soaking my shirt.

"You could have had a very large paycheck today Emery, but instead you chose to try stopping us. News flash, idiot, you will never stop us." Rossi spat at me.

He was right. No matter how hard I pushed it would never be enough.

It was no different trying to stop the sun from rising in the morning.

I locked my gaze on him.

"Doesn't matter. I'm not going to stop." I told him over the noise.

I watched him closely. His hand tightened around the grip of the pistol.

I could feel him getting ready to shoot and wondered what it would feel like, wondered if it would feel like last time.

Searing hot pain followed by the dreams then darkness.

But it wasn't going to happen.

Rossi jerked the trigger. The gun roared in his hands but the shot hit the engine behind me stopping it dead.

As I moved he yanked the trigger again.

And nothing. Just a dull click.

Rossi looked at the pistol in confusion.

I stepped forward with the knife held low in front of me.

Rossi eyed it and as he looked down he saw why the gun had failed.

The magazine was lying on the floor of the boat; it hadn't locked home.

The blade came up moving across in a vicious arc, the tip digging deep into his fleshy cheek.

He stepped back howling in pain.

I lunged forward driving the blade deep into his shoulder and slammed him back into the dashboard of the boat.

The scream pierced the darkness. Rossi looked at me, hatred in his eyes.

Carefully I slipped the pistol from its holster with my left hand.

"Go to hell Emery." Rossi spat.

I looked at him as I jammed the muzzle of the Beretta into his side then pulled the trigger three times spraying the white deck with blood.

Slowly he dropped to the floor. Not moving.

The spot light beam played over the boat.

I slipped the pistol into the holster and killed the engines but left the ignition on.

The fuel line for one of the engines was exposed; my knife slipped through it and fuel sprayed me in the face then began to flood the deck.

Mack slipped closer, a new rope hanging from the side of the helicopter. He swooped in swinging the rope to me. It took a moment longer than normal to knot the rope and to be lifted clear of the boat.

Mack climbed a hundred feet with me dangling below.

I looked up to see Dan peering down at me. I gave him a nod and he disappeared inside. The chopper banked towards the coast as Dan's arm came out holding a flare gun. He carefully aimed it at the boat and squeezed the trigger.

A bright red blob sailed out of the helicopter and hit the boat square in its centre.

It exploded into a huge fireball engulfing it in intense flames.

CHAPTER 55

Mack touched the AS350 down on the pad outside the hanger at the airport just as the first rays of sunshine began to lighten the eastern horizon. I sat with my back to the hanger door looking west towards the city. My watch said it was five thirty.

My head hurt and I couldn't move my left arm anymore without feeling like I would pass out.

The screaming of the turbine died away to reveal birds singing in the dawn light. Calum stepped from the helicopter as the blades spooled down; he walked around the front then opened the rear doors for everyone to climb out.

He reached inside and lifted Amy out to carry her into the hanger.

Dan walked towards me and looked down.

"How are you feeling?" He asked.

Mack and Melissa crowded around.

"Like I've been beaten up by a seven foot monster." I croaked.

I carefully touched my left side and winced.

Mack and Dan reached down to lift me to my feet.

My head swam and the world went dark.

I woke up.

Fluorescent lights hung from the ceiling casting a harsh glow around me.

Slowly I sat up.

There was no one in the room with me.

Night time had fallen over the world again.

I gazed around the room and noticed a newspaper sitting on the bed next to me. It was folded back to a page then folded in half and in quarter to isolate a section of the page. I looked down at it and read the headline.

AUCKLAND COP DEAD.

The article was short and to the point. It didn't tell me a lot. The unnamed officer had been travelling late at night over the Kaimais, along a particularly treacherous piece of road. The article blamed the conditions for the accident. The car had missed a corner completely then ploughed through a wire rope barrier plunging off a cliff into the bush below.

What was puzzling to the investigators was the apparent lack of skid marks on the tarseal. It was as if he didn't touch the brakes at all.

"Damn shame that." A voice called from the doorway.

I looked up.

Calum was leaning against the doorjamb.

I dropped the paper on the bed and sighed.

"I have no idea what you're talking about." I told him.

THE END.